WARY IS HER LOVE

SCHOOL OF NECESSARY MAGIC BOOK THREE

JUDITH BERENS   MARTHA CARR   MICHAEL ANDERLE

DISRUPTIVE IMAGINATION

Thanks to the JIT Readers

James Caplan
John Ashmore
Peter Manis
Daniel Weigert
Micky Cocker
Larry Omans
Paul Westman
Tim Bischoff

If we've missed anyone, please let us know!

A lison sat at a small round table across from Shay Carson at the South Central Avenue Starbucks in the center of Los Angeles. It was a hot and muggy day in California, and Alison couldn't wait to get back to Virginia. She was ready to get back to school and see her friends.

"It's not the heat, it's the humidity." She sipped her iced matcha lemonade.

"Good thing you can't see the green color," said Shay, wrinkling her nose.

Alison laughed and stuck out her green tongue. She looked at the different souls milling around the coffee shop, some magical, some not. Shay touched the back of Alison's hand.

"Did you have a good summer?"

Alison sat up and smiled. "I did. It was full of surprises."

"I can imagine." Shay laughed. "You learned martial arts. I bet you didn't see that one on your summer vacation list when you left school last year."

"No, but it was really cool of Dad to take time to teach me."

Shay smiled and looked down. "It's still so odd to hear you call Brownstone 'Dad.' I mean, it's fantastic, but it still throws me off a bit."

"It's nice to be able to call someone Dad whom I can look up to, and after he wanted to adopt me, well, it just kind of came naturally. I guess I've wanted a dad, even if I didn't admit it to myself."

"Well, now you have a good one, and you still have all the wonderful memories of your mother too."

"The best." Alison smiled, slurping the lemonade through a straw. "Thank you so much for taking me to your warehouse so I could work out. Those exercises to help my spatial awareness of souls and energy really broadened things for me."

"Good, that was the point. Now you can go back to school with those inner eyes wide open, able to kick some serious butt."

Alison laughed. "It'll make it so much easier now that I finally decided to 'fess up and tell everyone I have my own unique way of *seeing*." She looked up when she heard the bell on the door and Brownstone hurried over to them. "Sorry I'm late. Should we grab a coffee before we go?"

"That would be fantastic," Shay replied, standing up.

"Got mine!" Alison held up her matcha lemonade.

"What? Why are you drinking grass?"

"Millennial lemonade," explained Shay.

Alison smiled at Brownstone and stood up as she put on her bookbag. Brownstone grabbed her suitcase and headed to the counter.

"Double shot of espresso," he told the barista. "What do you want?" Shay ordered chai tea with a splash of soy milk.

They collected their drinks at the end of the counter and followed the line of magical commuters heading down the hall toward the bathroom, and kept walking right through the hidden magic wall at the back. They emerged on the metal platform above the intersecting staircases, and Alison moved over to the right side, gripping the railing with one hand and her lemonade with the other.

"Ready?" asked Brownstone, his hand in the small of her back, easily guiding her toward the stairs.

A Light Elf in baggy jeans and an old Pearl Jam t-shirt, his dark hair braided down his back, started at the sight of Brownstone. He made an abrupt about-face and faded back into the crowd. "Can't go anywhere these days," he muttered, hunching his shoulders.

"One of your prospects?" asked Shay, sizing up the tall, lanky young elf. She could still see his head above most of the crowd as he darted a nervous glance back at them.

"An informant who gave me a bad piece of intel. I'll catch up with him at a later date."

"Take a break, Dad. Summer's not quite over."

They headed for the staircase as Alison's hand glided over the top. She looked over her shoulder at Shay. "Remember what I said. You can see me off, but neither of you can touch the train. Only magical beings can touch it. You guys would go up in smoke. Poof! Like a cloud of ash."

Shay smiled and winked at Brownstone. "She's looking after us."

Brownstone snickered. "Not what I usually inspire in people."

Shay nudged him. "Our hands will stay away from the train, we promise."

They made their way down the staircases, pausing at several platforms where other staircases intersected. Each led to trains heading all over the world. People hurried off to different destinations, swinging backpacks and brief-cases. Alison glanced at their souls and wondered. Some were light greens and blues or a powerful red, while others had a hidden stream of dark magic swirling in the center.

She moved closer to the rail as a witch passed her, looking away from the black swirl.

The platform rattled as a train passed underneath. Brownstone cleared his throat and put his large hand on Alison's shoulder as they walked across it to descend another set of stairs. Alison smirked, knowing what was coming.

Brownstone frowned, not seeing his daughter's expression. "While we have a few minutes, I wanted to check with you on some things."

Shay sighed. "Please don't lecture her the rest of the way. We want her to come back to us next summer."

Brownstone ignored her comment. "You are a sopho-more now, and I know there has been at least one boy that you've liked."

"You know very well that she is still talking to Tanner." Shay arched an eyebrow, smirking. "Don't beat around the bush."

"Always keep at least one foot on the ground."

"What does that mean? You realize you're talking about magical teenagers. They would take that as a challenge." Shay stepped aside to let a wizard slide by her.

"Okay, keep both legs together. I know teenagers that age…"

"Only when you're hunting them, bounty hunter."

Alison let out a short laugh and put up her hand for a high-five from Shay.

"And they think they can get away with anything, especially when they are alone…"

"OKAY." Shay sighed. "Move on. New topic."

"You really should only be thinking about your studies at this point. What you do in this school can help determine what you become later in life. You could be a mercenary, a banker, a professor, a magic hunter…anything you want. But you have to study. With your abilities, I think you would make a fantastic detective for the magical sector of the government."

Shay interrupted, "You really *have* morphed into her dad. Can she get past her second year before she decides on the rest of her life?"

"Right. Anyway, get what you can out of the school. You have the rest of your life to hang out with friends."

Shay leaned forward and whispered in her ear, "Have some fun. The rest will fall into place. Life has a way of doing that."

She looked up at Brownstone, who tried his best not to smile and failed. "Some tomb raider. You sounded almost Zen."

"So shoot me. I've learned a few things. Isn't that what we do? Pass it along?"

Brownstone saw a young wizard smile at Alison as he crossed a different platform, inspiring him to start up again.

Alison kept walking down the stairs, nodding and smiling and sipping her green lemonade. Shay continued to do her best to change the subject, but Alison didn't really mind. Her biological father had been the worst person on Earth; he had tried to sell her to an Asian gang. Brownstone had not only rescued her but had also gone out of his way to do right by her. She could nod her way through a few lectures.

She stepped off the stairs and walked over to stand in front of the shiny red train. Brownstone set her bag down and took a deep breath, still talking. "And listen to the headmistress. Stay out of the kemana unless necessary. There is a lot of dark magic being practiced right now, and I don't want you caught in any crossfires. You've already been through enough."

"Okay, okay." Shay swatted Brownstone. "You better give her a hug before she completely misses her train and you are still standing here giving her advice when winter break comes."

Brownstone pulled her in for a tight hug. She smiled with her head against his chest, thankful for her new life. She pulled back, and Shay grinned at her, putting her hands on her shoulders.

"Be safe, and please don't listen to this boring old man. Say hello to Izzie for us and go have fun with your friends. Make memories."

Alison laughed and hugged Shay, feeling the warmth of her human energy. "I'll miss you guys."

"We'll miss you too." Shay sighed. "Now, go on, get on the train and get a good seat before the whole thing fills up."

Alison grabbed her bag and climbed on board, finding her way to the first seats on the right. She scooted across the empty seat to the window and looked out at Brownstone's and Shay's swirling energy. She smiled, seeing the hues of sadness swirling through Brownstone's, but she also knew he was doing his best to maintain his serious look. She waved goodbye as the train started to inch forward. Suddenly it took off with a *whoosh*, blowing Shay's hair back, leaving them standing alone on the platform.

Alison settled in, putting her bag next to her and looked around at the magical energy all around her. The whole train was lit up with vibrant energy. The train moved fast, pushing her back against the seat.

"Arriving in Kansas City, Missouri. Stand clear of the doors. Next stop, Charlottesville, Virginia." The doors opened, and commuters rushed out as others waited impatiently, ready to stream inside. The trains made it possible for commuters to live a thousand miles from work and still get there in under an hour. People stood in the aisles and held onto the handrails attached to the ceiling as the train started up again. It made a few sharp turns and climbed for a while before slowly descending into the Charlottesville underground stop. It only took a matter of minutes to go the entire distance across the country.

"Please watch the doors. Stopping in Charlottesville, Virginia. Next stop, Boston, Massachusetts," the announcer's voice blared overhead.

Alison gathered her bags and headed off, following the swirling colors of the souls ahead of her. They started rising, so she knew there were stairs in front of her. She climbed the stairs, running her hand over the railing, taking what was becoming a very familiar path. She got close to the first platform and looked up, recognizing several souls ahead. She smiled widely and waved her hand in the air.

"Peter, Ethan, Aya, Kathleen!"

They all leaned over the side. "Hello! What took you so long?"

"We were gonna send out a gargoyle to look for you."

"Ethan, we were not."

"We came halfway down the stairs to meet you."

She got to the platform and hugged each one, happy to see them. "Feels like it's been forever. Facetiming isn't the same. I missed you all! How was your summer?"

"The best." Kathleen sighed, smiling.

"I just can't believe we are sophomores now!" Aya cheered.

"Hey, and that doesn't come without its perks," Peter replied. "We can now get passes to the kemana."

"We can go legit!" said Ethan.

Aya grimaced. "I don't know if that's something I will be rushing to do after last year."

Alison smiled, and Aya took her hand, squeezing it. "It's a new year, which means we can start over."

The students and parents packed the platform as they

made their way up to head to the University of Virginia or the School of Necessary Magic.

The line moved slowly, one step at a time, but Alison and the others were too busy chatting about their classes to even notice. When they reached the top, they walked through the hidden opening into the Starbucks located on the mall in downtown Charlottesville. The smell of chocolate wafted over them, and Aya slipped away to order a drink from the counter. The others stood to the side, waiting for her as they looked around the crowded coffee house.

Alison could sense all the souls and the energy coursing from elves and gnomes, and the different witches and wizards' wands, carefully hidden away, but always within reach, just in case.

"Where is Emma?" Alison asked, noticing the fragrant smell of Kathleen's perfume.

"Oh, her parents wanted to bring her directly to the school. I think they conjured a portal this year. Magical world's idea of first-class travel. My parents would have done it—they hate the train—but they couldn't make it this year. I told them just to put me on the train; I could use the time to read."

Alison laughed. "Hopefully you didn't need too much time. It only took me twelve minutes to get from Los Angeles to Virginia on the red line."

"Took me thirty-two minutes from Paris, but by the time I got settled in, it was time to get unsettled."

"I'm sure." Alison smirked.

"All right, guys." Aya walked over with her iced white mocha. "We can go catch the bus now."

Alison searched the crowd for Ethan's and Peter's souls and found them sitting at a table, surrounded by a crowd of graduate students from UVA, some of them alumni of the School of Necessary Magic. Kathleen smiled at a silver-haired elf who had cut his hair and spiked it on top. "I might go to UVA next," she announced dreamily.

"That guy won't still be there, you know," said Peter.

"I haven't even thought about college." Alison looked at the UVA crowd. "I feel like I'm just starting to understand high school."

2

"Did you guys learn any cool magic this summer?" Ethan asked, facing the others as he backed out the door of Starbucks.

"No, just enjoyed my time in Paris," Kathleen replied.

"I tried some new Earth Magic spells; even mixed in a few old gadgets. Found a VHS player online and did some pretty interesting things with it. Only blew something up like four times this summer," Peter declared proudly.

Kathleen snorted. "I'm surprised your parents don't send you to camp."

"Wow, moving up in the world." Aya laughed.

"Well, I learned a new spell. Doesn't do anything spectacular, but I thought it was cool." Ethan slid his wand to the tip of his shirt sleeve, looking around as they passed a group of humans.

"I don't know if you should do that," Aya warned. "We aren't on vacation anymore, and you know the rules."

"I know, no magic when *normies* are around. Meh, have

a little fun," Ethan scoffed. "Besides, we aren't actually off vacation until we set foot on school grounds."

Aya cringed as Ethan bit his lip and flicked his wrist, sending a spiral of white light from his wand. It floated over the sidewalk, sizzled, then disappeared.

The school emblem appeared in front of Ethan on the sidewalk, lighting up with every step he took. Little crests formed one right after the other, invisible to the normies. Aya was about to congratulate him when the ground shook slightly under their feet.

The group stopped and looked at each other, momentarily worried. Slowly, a small crack opened along the concrete, and the ground started to crumble in front of them. Aya grabbed Ethan's sleeve and tugged.

"Stop it, turn it off."

Ethan looked wide-eyed at the ground and back at Aya. "I don't know how. I only learned how to cast it, not counter-cast it. That class is this semester." He groaned.

"Oh, two moons!" Kathleen winced, backing up from the crumbling concrete.

The spidery crack worked its way toward two middle-aged witches and a wizard, who had grim faces as they pushed their way through the crowd. The witch in the middle flicked her wand, creating a bubble around them that shielded them from the view of the normies. The wizard swirled his wand and the normies detoured around them without even realizing it.

Quickly the group cast a spell in unison, stopping the concrete from breaking apart any farther. The witch in the center swirled her wand over her head, spreading a blanket of light across the ground. The teenagers watched wide-eyed as all the crumbled pieces knitted themselves back into place and the concrete sealed itself back together.

When the sidewalk was mended, the witch released the shield and the three glared at the group with their hands on their hips. The woman in the middle, an older witch, arched an eyebrow at Ethan. Ethan slid his wand back up his sleeve and kicked at the ground, embarrassed.

"I know you've been away from school for a while, but you are back and in our town. We have successfully kept this place quiet for decades."

The wizard firmly nodded his head. "We would appreciate it if you showed some restraint and responsibility when you are here. The headmistress would have all of you cleaning bathrooms by hand for a year if she knew you were casting in a public space. No magic, actual scrubbing!"

The younger witch, who had been quiet, patted the man on the back and smirked. "Oh, lighten up. I remember what it was like to be a teenager and own a wand, and I'm pretty sure you do too. What was that wand, a dogwood? You must be from around these parts."

The wizard nodded curtly at the kids and walked off with the older witch; the younger witch winked at the teenagers as she caught up with her friends. Alison and her friends were starting out with an adventure, barely avoiding trouble on their first day back at school.

Aya stood next to Alison at the bus stop and squeezed her elbow. Alison smiled, sensing the excitement in Aya's soul.

She was just as happy to be back as Alison was. "Kathleen looks a little lost," whispered Aya.

"I would be too if I had spent the entire summer in the streets of Paris, eating cheese, drinking wine, and looking at art."

Aya giggled. "Staring at boys."

"This place might not be so exciting for her anymore."

"Here comes the jitney," Ethan said with a weary sigh. "Back to reality."

Aya laughed and patted him on the shoulder. "Cheer up. It won't be so bad. We aren't freshmen anymore, and you have months to plan for April Fool's Day."

He smiled, perking up a little as the bus came to a stop in front of them. The driver opened the doors, and one by one they climbed aboard. Alison followed Aya to the middle of the bus and squeezed in next to her. She put her suitcase by her feet and slid her backpack off, placing it on her lap. The bus lurched forward, picking up speed, and headed toward the school.

They rolled by the University, students running across campus to greet their friends, and parents nervously sending their grown kids off for their first year of college. Others played frisbee on the Lawn.

They wove down the winding road, passing expansive horse farms with southern-style mansions perched atop rolling green hills. They turned onto a narrow road that ran under the canopy created by the overhanging branches of the old-growth oak trees bordering both sides of the pavement. Alison could smell the fresh-cut grass and horse farms from the partially open window in front of her. It was familiar and comforting, and she felt all the tension and anxiety start to melt away.

The bus slowed to a stop in front of the large wrought iron gates with the crest of the school welded to the top. Alison stood up, slung on her backpack, grabbed her case, and followed the rest of the students off the bus and out onto the road.

The bus had to make several trips to pick up more students from the Starbucks, and it carefully turned around and bounced back down the curving road.

Aya and Kathleen walked on either side of Alison, following Peter and Ethan as they went through the arch onto the school grounds. The courtyard was packed with students, the newbies on the right surrounded by their parents and all their things, and the older students on the left, talking excitedly about their summers. Peter lifted an eyebrow and looked back at the girls.

"I'm so glad I'm *not* a newbie anymore. I don't know if I could take another year of practical jokes from the upper-classmen."

Aya looked at the frightened expressions on the fresh-man's faces. "Did we look that nervous our first day?"

"I know I didn't," Kathleen replied. "But I remember very well a nervous-as-hell expression on your poor little face the first time I saw you."

Alison looked at the souls milling about to find Izzie's familiar energy, but she didn't see her anywhere. She knew that Izzie was already here, since she had stayed at the school with Headmistress Berens. Alison sighed, figuring she was inside getting the room ready or something.

A group of juniors stood by one of the old oak trees in

the courtyard talking about their summer vacations. "I had an internship at one of the banks in the kemana."

"That's lucky," a girl responded. "I had an internship with my father at a marketing firm for humans. Talk about boring."

"I went to Oriceran for several weeks, and then Sanibel Island back here on Earth to enjoy the beach. I'll do my internship next summer."

"I worked at the Dairy Queen in Tappahannock trying to save money," another responded. "It sucked, but at least I'm not dead broke this year."

Alison's group walked through the center of the courtyard toward the front doors. Amelia, the girl's dorm manager, waved at them, excusing herself from a conversation with one of the nervous parents. The girls stopped and smiled, and Emma joined them, nudging Aya.

"Ladies," Amelia said. "It's so good to see you. You all looked rested and ready to start a new year."

"We are." Emma smiled. "Are we in the same dorm as last year?"

"Oh, yes, you are. You'll stay there until you graduate. That reminds me, the headmistress is looking for all of you. She wanted to see you in her office as soon as you arrived."

The girls looked nervously at each other, and Kathleen wrinkled her nose. "Any idea why?"

"I don't really know. Something about the condition of your room," Amelia replied distractedly, waving at one of the professors. "Just go ahead over there; she's waiting, I have to help direct the freshmen."

The girls smiled and nodded, exchanging curious looks.

None of them had any idea what it was about, but they were not looking forward to finding out.

The girls stood in the wide entryway of the school talking to some of the other students. Alison was still looking around for Izzie, but her friend was nowhere to be found. Neither was Tanner, but they had barely exchanged texts or calls over the summer. Alison had been so busy with her training that she only occasionally thought about him.

"Hey, ladies." Professor Fowler smiled, her red hair in a messy, frizzy bun on the top of her head. "Headmistress Berens wanted to see you before you settled in."

"Yeah." Emma sighed. "We are about to go to her office."

Professor Fowler nodded and walked quickly off, frantic energy swirling around her.

Kathleen looked at the other girls and shrugged. "We might as well just get it over with."

They made their way down the hall and stopped outside of Headmistress Berens' office. Kathleen glanced at the others, shaking her head.

"Don't look guilty already. We don't even know what this is about."

"Can't be anything good," Emma grumbled.

Kathleen raised her chin and straightened her back as she faced the ornate doors in front of her. She lifted her hand, but before she could knock, Headmistress Berens called out.

"Come on in, girls. Don't just stand in the hall."

Kathleen shook her head and glanced at the others, not

sure how the headmistress managed to do that every time. She opened the door and the girls took one step inside, bunched together nervously. The headmistress put some papers in the filing cabinet and looked at them.

"All the way. I won't bite."

They stepped in farther. Alison closed the door and walked up next to Aya's nervous energy. Headmistress Berens sat down behind her desk and tapped her fingers, glancing at Izzie, who sat in a corner chair looking more than unhappy. Alison leaned forward, sensing Izzie's presence, and smiled sweetly at her.

"I am wondering exactly what happened to your room, because when we went in this morning to deliver linens, it was torn up from top to bottom."

The girls glanced at each other. "Maybe it was the squirrel that was in the boy's dorm last year."

"Right, so a mad squirrel got into the mansion without setting off any of our spell alarms, went up the stairs—specifically to your room—closed the door behind it, completely ravaged the space, and then dove out the closed window into the yard?"

Kathleen sighed and rolled her eyes, raising her hand. "We found an egg at the beginning of last year,, so we brought it back to the room."

"It hatched?" Emma asked excitedly.

"We thought it was dead or petrified or something," Kathleen added.

Alison and Izzie kept their mouths shut. They had felt the life force in that egg, and knew very well that it had not been dead. "I thought you put it in the barn?" Alison whispered to Izzie.

"I did, but I was afraid, so I put it back in your drawer before I left and closed the door. I figured it would be fine."

"Well, that was not only reckless but completely against the rules." Mara sighed. "Now, I will let you in on a little secret. I knew the entire time you had that egg up there."

"You did?" Emma asked. "Why didn't you say something?"

"I wanted you girls to learn the lesson on your own," she said sternly. "Normally this could get you suspended, but I gather from the astounded looks on your faces, that you did. Nonetheless, you will be responsible for cleaning up the dining hall for the next week... at every meal."

The girls groaned, but Mara held a hand up, silencing them. "Maybe next time you will know not to bring random creatures up to your rooms. Now, go on, get settled in and join us for dinner. Yes, you will be cleaning up tonight."

Mara looked down but glanced up as the girls sulked out of the room, trying to hide a smirk.

3

Izzie walked to the dorm room door and took a deep breath, then pushed it open. She had been there when they found the disaster, but hadn't seen it since Mara had gone in and fixed the damage.

The girls filed into the room and looked around, dropping their suitcases beside them. Most of the damage had already been repaired, except for a few scratches on the side of the desk and rake-marks along the closet doors.

"Those claw marks are too big to be a squirrel, that's for sure."

"Maybe a really big raccoon. That was what we should have said."

"She already knew. It was a dragon. Yeah, a dragon..."

The marks definitely belonged to a young dragon, which didn't surprise any of them.

Izzie looked at Emma and tapped her on the shoulder. "Could we switch beds? I'd kind of like to be near Alison."

Emma smiled in understanding and nodded. The girls

started to unpack and put their things away, not saying much to each other. Shay had helped Alison pack so she would know exactly where everything was, and the girl lined it up perfectly in the closet on her own. When they were all done, Izzie sat on the edge of her bed waiting for Kathleen.

"I think we should go look for the dragon," Kathleen said, surprising everyone. "What? I didn't agree to keep that egg in the drawer all semester last year and have it wreck our room not to get a good look at it after it hatched."

"Yay, brilliant idea!" Emma cheered.

"Haven't you seen it, Izzie?"

"The headmistress had me staying with her in the mansion, and it was hard to get away without her noticing." She held up her hands, shrugging. "I had no idea about our room. She kept that one to herself, but it explains all the looks I got."

They hurried to put away their empty cases and headed out. Aya shut the door behind them. They threaded through the masses of students and parents who were still gathered in the entryway saying their anxious goodbyes.

The girls crossed the courtyard, ignoring the stares of Claire and Scarlett as they marched through. Once they crested the hill, Izzie latched arms with Alison and squeezed her hand.

"So good to see you. Sorry I couldn't meet you guys when you got here. Headmistress Berens was holding me prisoner until she talked to you guys."

"It's all right. I'm just glad to see you." Alison smiled.

"We should start down at the stream where we found

it," Kathleen yelled, taking off across the fields for the woods.

They picked their way through the brush and down to the creek, walking over to the edge of the gulley. They were disappointed as they stared at a pile of rocks and stones covering the entrance to the cave. Aya put her hands on her hips and narrowed her eyes.

"It looks like someone did that on purpose."

"Probably the headmistress," Kathleen guessed. "Probably smart, though, because any clueless freshman could fall into the cave, never to be seen again."

"Well, what about the other side of the forest?" Emma asked. "Or maybe in the orchard? There's probably still fruit on the trees."

Kathleen shrugged. "Might as well give it a shot. Get in a little fun before we turn into maids."

"I wonder if they'll let us use magic?" mused Aya.

The other girls shook their heads at her in unison.

Alison and Izzie wanted to see the dragon, even though they were enjoying the nice cool breeze that blew through the canopy of the trees. They headed back out of the woods, everyone stopping in their tracks as they hit the tree line. Horace looked at them with a smirk and a raised eyebrow.

"Well, look who it is…all my troublemakers."

Izzie smiled broadly and waved. "Hey, Horace!"

Horace nodded at her and tapped his foot on the ground. "What could the five of you be doing out here just after you got back?"

"Just going for a walk?" Kathleen choked out.

"Right, a nice leisurely walk through the woods? That

might have been believable from, say, Izzie and Alison, but you, Kathleen?" He tilted his head to the side. "Try again."

"We're looking for the dragon," Izzie blurted.

The others looked at her. "What? It's obvious he knows we're up to something."

"Ahh, that little fellow. Yeah, I've been keeping an eye on him since his mad dash from your dorm room. Have you named him yet?"

"Hardly," Kathleen grumbled. "We haven't even *seen* him yet."

"It's a he," squealed Emma.

"He's in the cooler parts of the forest near a small cave. There is a lot of small game over there, which is perfect for him right now. He has quite the appetite, and they grow really fast during this period. Since he isn't too fond of the hot weather, he spent several days in the dampness of the cave. He's okay, though. I made sure of that for you. I figured you would be worried once you got back."

Emma smiled excitedly. "What does he look like? Does he have a personality?"

Horace laughed and rubbed the back of his sunburnt neck. "He's a plump little guy, with bluish-grey scales that shimmer in the sunlight. He's a Silver Dragon, which from what I've heard is very rare, especially on Earth. In fact, he might be the only one on Earth. Mara said you can barely ever find one on Oriceran, and that's if you are really looking for them. I'm not sure how you got your hands on one, but we are hoping he stays here on the property when he gets older. You know, so that we can watch out for him."

"That's so strange." Aya shook her head. "If they are so

rare, and he's the only one on Earth, how did his egg get here?"

Horace's face went serious. "I don't know. That seems to be the question of the day, but you found him, and that's what's important for now. He didn't like being cooped up in your room so much, though." He chuckled. "He really did a number on the place. Pulled all the feathers out of your comforters and spread them out like snow over the whole room. I couldn't help but smile when I saw it."

"I don't think the headmistress shared your sentiment," Kathleen muttered.

"What are Silver Dragons like?" Alison asked, sensing Horace's comfortable human soul.

"From what I found out, they like to be near humans, or at least the ones they know they can trust. Throughout time they've been known to be very protective of the innocent, though they don't go out looking for danger. If they happen to come upon it, though, they won't hesitate to jump in and save the day." He pulled out a small switchblade, flipped it open, and scooped up a block of balsa wood, whittling the edges.

"They are very honorable creatures, not to mention extraordinarily intelligent, and that can't be said for most dragons. There have been tales from Oriceran, from long before the Light Elf kingdom was established. Silver Dragons actually sat on the councils of the various lands, helping to protect the place from enemies."

"What happened to them?" Aya asked.

"I'm not sure. They are very curious, especially when they are young; not much different than a human child. They're kind to every creature they meet unless they feel threatened, but something in the past was able to push them out of mainstream life, and even where they usually congregated, you'd be lucky to find a footprint." He pressed down with the edge of the knife and cut out a small curve. "Whoever had this egg must have hidden it well. The eggs are very precious to the species, which is probably why it was brought to Earth. The others would have searched it out on Oriceran."

"You sure know a lot about dragons for a human." Kathleen shaded her eyes with her hand and tried to peer into the trees.

"They interest me, I guess. But this guy...man, he is adorable! Come on, I'll take you to see him."

The girls followed Horace into the shaded part of the forest, through the overgrown vines and fallen trees into a clearing. To the right was a small dark cave, the rocks sparkling with silver flecks.

Alison stared at the energy coming from the cave and couldn't help but wonder if it was somehow connected to the kemana. It glowed like it should be. Horace walked ahead of them, putting his hand out to stop them.

He bent down on one knee and whistled loudly, and two yellow eyes brightened the darkness. Horace smiled and put out his hands, and the small pudgy dragon leapt from the cave and ran happily into Horace's arms. He petted his scaly head, and jerked backward as the dragon's tail nearly swiped across his face.

"Whoa, little buddy, calm down. I brought you some visitors. They're old friends of yours."

The dragon tilted his head, looked behind Horace, and jumped out of his lap. He stepped forward and sat down, taking his time to look each of the girls in the eyes. Alison watched the wild energy flow around him, the same spiraling colors that had been inside the egg.

"Hey there, buddy." Izzie smiled. "We thought you were going to wait to hatch until we got there."

Aya laughed. "Yeah, you caused quite the ruckus inside the mansion.

"He is the most adorable thing I have ever seen." Emma giggled.

The dragon's eyes brightened and he ran up to them, recognizing their voices. "Momma! I missed you all! Where have you been?"

Izzie let out a snort of laughter and covered her mouth. "He...he sounds like us!"

"He thinks we're his momma?" asked Alison, laughing.

"I believe you girls are all his mother." Horace scratched his beard with the edge of his knife, smiling. "Little fella must have bonded with your voices inside his egg. Even learned how to talk. I reckon he sounds just like..."

"A teenage girl!" blurted Emma, laughing.

The dragon opened his mouth and let out a low rumble and a laugh, cold air blowing out of his nose. He rubbed against Kathleen's leg, and she arched an eyebrow. "Too soon, scaly dude." She looked at Horace as the other girls petted him, laughing when he rolled over on his back.

"Does he fly?" Kathleen asked.

"Not yet. He's too young. He's only about three feet long at this point, but let me tell you—he eats *a lot*."

"Probably gets that from me." Izzie patted her belly.

"What should we do with him?" Emma asked. "It's obvious he doesn't like the room, and we couldn't put him back into the cave even if it weren't blocked off. No sign of any other dragons around that could have laid that egg."

"Thank goodness," murmured Kathleen.

Emma continued, "And the grounds of the school are protected by spells. No indication of who could have gotten onto the grounds and left the egg."

"All good points, ladies. What say we recognize this is a wild animal with a pointy tail and do very little? Let Mother Nature have a shot at it." A small dragon started to emerge from the block of wood Horace was whittling. "A silver dragon is designed to take care of itself, and I'll keep an eye on him. You ladies have big hearts, but you're not to forget—he may be smart and sweet and see you as his clan, but he is still a dragon. He's out there hunting for small prey at night and chomping down."

The girls wrinkled their noses in unison.

"Eventually he will have a wingspan that will put a nice bit of shade over your heads."

"Sheesh," Izzie replied, rubbing the little guy's face.

"For now, the safest thing to do is leave him right here."

"Come and visit," the dragon called as he crept back into the shadows.

"That is creepy," said Kathleen, shaking her head. "He sounds just like one of us."

4

After all the parents had left, clothes were hung, and freshmen were settled, the entire student body made their way to the dining hall for their first dinner together. After visiting the dragon, the girls had enough time to get cleaned up and change into something appropriate for cleanup duty.

"Better the headmistress doesn't know where we've been," Kathleen said, putting out her hand for the others to lay theirs on top. "All for one..."

Inside the cafeteria everyone chatted loudly, cheering at different displays of magic and happy to be back together. The cavernous hall was filled with round tables and ladderback chairs with paper placemats in front of each. The sconces gave off a magical blue light that flickered and a glow that was favorable to anyone.

Alison and her friends sat down at the same table as last year, and the girls immediately started gushing to Peter and Ethan about the dragon.

"Man, I wish we could have seen him," Peter said, leaning over the table so he could be heard.

"I'm just glad we didn't keep him in *our* room, not after the cleaning disaster at the end of the year." Ethan laughed, jabbing Peter in the ribs.

Peter turned bright red, glancing at Emma. Alison tried to make out the different conversations, but the mixture of voices was so loud that it was difficult to hear the others.

Up on the small stage located at the front of the great hall, Mara Berens sat next to Professor Eleanor Hudson, who lightly rubbed her forehead. She stood, pushed her round black glasses up her nose, and smoothed back her perfect, short blond hair. She cleared her throat and walked to the front of the stage, waving her wand over her head.

No one seemed to notice except the freshmen, who gawked at the dome of pale, calming light that slowly fell over the crowd. It gradually grew quiet as her spell separated the noise into different funnels so that people could only hear what was directed at them.

Kathleen sat back in her chair and let out a sigh, grateful not to have to strain anymore to hear the others. "I have an even better prank this year," yelled Ethan, caught off-guard by the spell. The whole group laughed as he winced, then shrugged it off.

Professor Hudson crossed her arms and pressed her lips together as she looked across the sea of students directly at Ethan.

"Gosh, Ethan, I haven't heard you scream that loud since you asked Grace to the dance." Kathleen laughed.

"I think I liked it better when I couldn't hear the cat-scratch of your voice, Kathleen," Ethan replied with narrowed eyes.

"Ah." Emma sighed, putting her hands in her lap. "It's good to be back to normal. I almost missed the bickering between the two of you."

Ethan made a face at Emma, and she giggled. "You are like the evil stepbrother I never wanted, but now that I have you, I wouldn't give you up for the world."

Alison turned to stare at the walls. She could see the glimmer of energy that ran around the cafeteria. They had spelled the place to look extra-special for the first day of school. Magical stars flickered on the curved ceiling high over their heads. Alison watched, entranced by the energy.

"What's the constellation on the ceiling?" she asked Izzie in a whisper.

"Oh, it's the night sky, including Oriceran's second moon. I read about it this summer. Not much to do, and Leo Decker let me check out almost any book. There're even blooming Oriceran flowers attached to vines that are constantly moving around the walls."

Izzie smiled, tilting her head back to gaze at the enchanted ceiling. Alison looked around the room at the excitement swirling in the souls, even recognizing Claire and Scarlett by the streaks of red shimmering in the middle. "I will be giving them some room this year," she muttered.

"What?" asked Izzie, looking away from the ceiling.

"Nothing."

Mara Berens took a sip of her tea and set the cup down on the saucer. She adjusted the colorful silk scarf neatly wrapped around her neck and walked to the apron of the stage, nodding at Professor Hudson.

Professor Hudson swished her wand, grimacing as the spell lifted and the loud voices filled the hall again. Everyone noticed the change and quickly quieted, turning in their chairs to look up at the headmistress. She put her hand up to her throat, and a bright glow on her palm soaked into her skin. When she spoke, her voice echoed around the room like a sound system.

"Welcome, students, to your first day back at the School of Necessary Magic. For those who are here for the first time, we hope you learn to love this school as much as we do. Now, you all have been given your general itineraries, which include meal times, different clubs, sports, and other social events that the school will be putting on. You also have a list of your individual class assignments for this semester, and if anyone has an issue, please see Professor Hudson in her office after dinner is concluded."

She cleared her throat and pulled a list out of her pocket, adjusting her glasses. She held the paper in front of her, squinted at the small print, and nodded with a smile when she found her place.

"Just a few notes for this school year. Freshmen are not permitted in the kemana *for any reason*. Sophomores are permitted but will need to have a permission slip signed by either myself or Professor Hudson, and will be allowed to go on a case by case basis. Any major infractions will see those privileges revoked, so I suggest you be on your best behavior. For those who don't know, the forest area behind the orchard is off-limits, as well as the gardens behind the Botanical buildings, without express written permission from Professor Fowler. There are some plants in there that require a bit of caution."

"You're telling me," Kathleen muttered.

"Also, after some of the events of last year, we are instituting a weekend curfew. The details will be posted outside, but you have to be back on the grounds by that time. This is for the safety of all the students, and will be enforced at least through winter break."

There was a collective groan from the upperclassmen in the corner. "Great, some idiot got crazy not knowing how to handle his magic, and now we're all being punished for it."

"It's not a punishment," Headmistress Berens said, glaring at Claire. "It's a safety measure, and that is all. Now, everyone enjoy your dinner, and welcome our incoming freshmen. Help them when they need it, and have a wonderful school year."

Several people clapped, and everyone went back to their conversations. Students sat with the friends they had made during their first year.

"I'm glad we're all still together," Alison said.

"Where's Luke?" Aya asked as her food appeared in front of her.

Izzie glanced at his empty chair as a pile of spaghetti appeared on her plate. Ethan swallowed a bite of his burger and wiped his mouth on his sleeve, making Kathleen grimace.

"He told me he would be back by the time classes start. He had something going on tonight."

"You know what I'm glad for?" Emma said excitedly.

"Food; real home-cooked food. Well, kind of home-cooked."

She closed her eyes and concentrated on her plate. Opening her eyes, she clapped at the crabmeat ravioli with rosé sauce that appeared in front of her. "When I grow up I want to use this spell in my house."

"Mmmm." Kathleen nodded, swallowing a mouthful of lettuce. "Me too. I hate cooking."

"Oh yeah, it takes so much effort to throw a salad and a carrot stick on a plate." Ethan snickered.

"At least I won't have clogged arteries from all the cheeseburgers," Kathleen retorted.

Alison agreed. She really liked being back and having the food at the school. "I ate barbeque and pizza all summer."

"Mara uses this spell at her house in Crozet, not far from here." Izzie shrugged.

Alison picked up a chicken finger from her plate, dipping it in the sauce to the side. She never cared too much about the food she ate every day, but she did like the fact that she could look forward to eating things that were really close to what her mother used to cook her. It felt good to have that connection still intact.

When she was finished eating she stared at the souls, wondering where Tanner was. When some new people came through the doorway, Tanner's shining soul was at the back of the crowd, with a small cloud of black deep inside still tugging at the light. She smiled and jumped from her seat, rushing over to give him a hug. He turned his face into her hair and took a deep breath of her strawberry shampoo, holding her tightly. She took his hand and pulled him back toward the table.

Ethan looked up and rolled his eyes. "Great, the toombie is coming to sit with us."

Last semester there had been a dark magic incident, and the whole school was on edge about toombies. Dark families took orphaned children, usually babies, and inserted a ball of dark magic into their souls. Everyone was pointing fingers these days at kids who didn't have families.

"Maybe we should talk to Alison about it," Kathleen whispered. "Seriously, one of us could be the next victim because we hang around him too much."

"I think it's the opposite. If he's the one, he won't want to hurt his friends." Emma shrugged.

"Everyone shush," Izzie whispered, leaning forward. "Do I need to remind you that everyone suspects both Alison and me of being toombies? Cut the guy a little slack. I'm sure that if Alison trusts him, we have nothing to worry about. Don't make him feel uncomfortable."

Alison sat down, pulling Tanner into the seat next to her. Izzie cleared her throat and smiled at Tanner. The rest of the table looked down at their food, pushing it around on their plates.

"Hey, Tanner," Izzie greeted him. "How was your summer?"

"Okay." He shrugged. "Quiet. I think that with all the rumors I kind of lost some of my friends."

"Well, they weren't friends to begin with, then. You are more than welcome here with us."

Alison squeezed Izzie's hand in thanks. By that point

dinner was wrapping up, and people started to get up and leave for the night. One by one the plates disappeared from the table as everyone stood. Tanner turned to Alison and took her hands.

"May I walk you back to your room?"

From behind them, they heard Mara Berens clear her throat. Izzie looked back as she nodded toward the cleaning supplies that magically appeared in the doorway. Alison shook her head.

"Not tonight. We kind of have cleanup duty for the next week."

"Uh oh, what did you guys do on your first day back?" Tanner laughed.

"Kind of a long story, but I'll tell you later."

Tanner nodded at Ethan and Peter as they waited for him by the door, then leaned in and kissed her on the cheek. The girls walked over and grabbed the different supplies, Izzie handing Alison a rag and a spray bottle. Kathleen struggled with the mop, blowing her hair out of her eyes.

"This is going to be a long week."

5

When they'd finally finished cleaning the cafeteria the non-magical way, they walked back up to their room, half-disheveled, and got ready for bed. Everyone else in the dorms was already in their room, and lights out came just fifteen minutes later. They didn't complain, though. They were all exhausted from the day— except Alison and Izzie, of course. Izzie laid on her side, facing Alison.

"Did you get any rest on vacation?" Izzie asked.

"Actually, I did. Brownstone was teaching me martial arts and Shay had me work out with her most days, so by the time night hit I was ready for meditation mode. I didn't even really dream while I was there or wander out of body or whatever it is that happens when I go into that state. I actually feel like I could go a few days without recharging. How about you? Did you get any sleep?"

"At first, no. I kept having the weirdest dreams about people I have never met before. I told Mara about it, and after that, she put a sleep spell on me every night. I slept like a baby, waking up in the same position as when I fell asleep. I think it's the most sleep I've had my whole life."

Alison smiled, running her hand over the sheet next to her. "I can't believe the dragon hatched while we were gone."

"I know." Izzie giggled. "You would have died if you'd seen Mara's face when she walked in here. Seriously it looked like we threw one hell of a party."

"I can imagine." Alison laughed. "But he is so sweet, and his energy is beautiful. I knew there wasn't going to be a bad bone in his body."

"He's adorable. I keep imagining him covered in feathers like a molting chicken." She chuckled.

"Maybe we should name him 'Cluck.'"

Both the girls covered their mouths, trying not to wake the others with their laughter. The other girls had just fallen asleep, and Izzie knew that if they woke Kathleen up, she would have some words to say. They waited until the laughter simmered down. Izzie sighed and turned over on her back.

"He is so round. I feel like we should put him on a diet or something."

"He'll grow out of it. I don't think we can put a dragon on a diet." Alison giggled again. "I can't wait until he starts to fly. Do you think we will be able to ride him?"

"That would be so cool," Izzie whispered excitedly. "The wind in our faces, high above the ground, soaring through the clouds. We could make a saddle for him and become fierce dragon warriors."

"Do they need those on Earth?"

Izzie chuckled. "I don't know. Maybe? It would be very cool."

She sat up and looked around the room, making sure the others were asleep. The girls quietly slipped on shoes and light jackets and tiptoed out of the room. Izzie wrinkled her nose as she carefully shut the door and the two girls made their way down the hall.

"You know we're breaking curfew," whispered Alison.

"I won't tell if you don't."

When they got to the stairs they stepped around the creaking areas, remembering where the exact spots were from the year before.

Downstairs was silent; everyone was tucked away in their beds. The girls made it outside and onto the grounds for the first night stroll of their sophomore year. Alison zipped up her jacket and took a deep breath of the country air. The nights were already starting to get a bit cold, so she was glad she had brought a jacket. The crisp air filled her lungs, bringing life back into her soul. Out of everything she'd missed about being there, these walks were number one on her list.

Izzie felt the same way. She always felt so free when she was out there. She had time to talk about anything on her mind, feel the cool air whip around her, and just *be*, even if it was for just a little while. She tilted her head back as they walked across the fields and looked at the beautiful clear night sky, which was even more beautiful than the dining hall's representation.

A shooting star darted across the heavens, and she closed her eyes, making a wish. When she opened them she wrinkled her forehead. She wasn't sure where she had gotten wishing on a star from, but it felt like something she'd done a thousand times.

"I see Horace's soul ahead," Alison whispered.

Izzie looked at the top of the hill. He sat on a wobbly old wooden stool, several lanterns around him and a blanket on the ground in front of him. He was polishing something that looked like a part for one of the many farm tools on the property. As the girls approached, he looked up and smiled.

"I figured I might see you out here tonight. First stroll of the year. I have to admit that I missed this."

"We did too." Alison smiled, sitting down on the blanket.

Izzie sat next to her and looked at the horizon, the last of the fireflies sparkling in the distance. "Have you seen the dragon?"

"This morning I did, I took him some raw eggs as a treat. And again, when I showed you girls where he was. It's best to leave him alone at night. That's when he goes hunting for food. Small game, mostly."

Izzie leaned back on her hands. "What did you do this summer?"

"I went to Texas to visit my Aunt Estelle," he replied. "It was fun. She had parties on the patio of her bar, and there were a lot of magical folks there. They really started flocking to the bar when Leira Berens left twenty years ago. I was glad to get back here, though. I missed the animals. How about you, Alison? What did you do?"

"I was officially adopted by James Brownstone, and I got the chance to learn martial arts," she recited, ticking the things off on her fingers.

"Nice. That's a lot," he said, surprised. "You got a family and you're a force to be reckoned with. And you, Izzie?"

"I just hung out here in Virginia with Mara. She created a magical pool for me in the backyard, so that was nice."

They stayed there talking about the school year, their vacations, and everything else for as long as they could. It was something all of them loved to do, and they were relieved to be back.

When the moon was about to disappear and the sky was beginning to lighten, the girls started back to the dorms. They were quiet most of the way, Izzie enjoying the air and Alison lost in her thoughts. When they reached the edge of the field, Alison grabbed Izzie's arm.

"What's wrong?" Izzie asked.

"Nothing. I just want to tell you something."

"Okay, I'm all ears."

"I've really been thinking about this a lot. This summer Shay worked with me to broaden my ability to see the energies and souls around me and react faster; become more agile. The martial arts training really helped. It's not only prepared me for whatever comes after we get out of high school, but given me confidence."

Alison took a deep breath and blew it out. "I'm going to relax about others knowing I'm blind. I don't want it to be a thing anymore."

"I get it. It's up to you, and I'll back you up, no matter what you decide."

Alison pushed a long strand of white hair off her shoulder. "When I was growing up, my mother tried to make me as independent as she could. She didn't want me to have to rely on others. I had no idea till last year that special sight sometimes appears in Drow, same time I found out I was a Drow. The only thing that has stopped me from telling is I don't want people to treat me differently, but the only way to make it not a thing is to own it."

"Mara says that a lot." Izzie smiled. "There's no shame in your game, that's for sure. You're my best friend, and you have done amazing things. Everyone loves you and knows how strong you are. I don't think anyone's opinion will change because they know you're blind. Besides, you see the world in a really cool way, and you helped save that kid last year. No one else could have done that, and it even saved Tanner. He would have been crushed if that student had died."

"True. I'm gonna do it."

Izzie smiled and reached out, taking her hand. She was about to say something but stopped, feeling in her gut something wasn't quite right. She dropped Alison's hand and looked around.

"Who's there?"

Leaves crunched on the edge of the courtyard, and a pair of bright amber-colored eyes gleamed at her from behind the tall green bushes bordering the walkway. A large wolf with brown and white fur stepped out and blocked their path.

Alison looked in the direction of the sound, recognized the shifter's energy, and instinctively pulled Izzie back, putting her arm up. Izzie stood her ground, entranced by the shifter's gaze, and pushed down on Alison's arm.

"Wait," she whispered, taking a step closer. The wolf's head was at the same height as Izzie's face.

Izzie recognized something in the wolf's eyes, and she stood there transfixed, her heart beating faster inside of her chest. She could barely hear anything besides her heart beat.

"It's Luke," she whispered, slowly raising her hand despite Alison's protests. His brown fur shimmered in the light of the moon. He panted hard, staring at Izzie, and sat down, holding her gaze.

"I know, but..." Alison could see the strength of the energy in front of her.

Izzie gently touched the fur just behind his ears.

"Izzie, what are you doing?" Alison looked in the direction of the mansion for the telltale energy of anyone else in the vicinity, but at this time of night, everyone was tucked in and fast asleep.

Izzie didn't look away from the large wolf. She started to smile, grateful that he was so calm.

Izzie tilted her head to the side. "Luke... It's okay. I'm here."

The wolf lowered his head and let Izzie rub the top, letting out a satisfied growl that vibrated right through Izzie's hand.

Izzie smiled, anxiety turning to butterflies in her stomach. "There's a connection between us. I knew it," she murmured softly. The wolf raised his head and looked at her. For a moment she felt like they were the only two beings in the world.

A howl erupted in the distance, and the wolf jerked his head around and shook his large body. Izzie snatched her hand away, taking several steps back. His ears turned in the direction of the sound, and he tilted his head back, answering the call.

The sound was deafening, and Alison squeezed Izzie's arm. "We need to go."

"In a moment," Izzie answered.

There was another howl from far away. The wolf turned back to look at Izzie before taking off at a run, disappearing into the forest as he ran toward his pack.

Izzie stood there, lost in what had happened. She had wondered all day where Luke was, and now she knew. Alison let go of Izzie's arm and patted her on the back, startling her. Izzie let out a deep breath and squeezed Alison's hand.

"Let's get inside before the headmistress wakes up and catches us," Alison whispered. "We're already cleaning the dining hall without magic. I don't want to find out what's next on her to-do list."

"Right," Izzie replied, still mesmerized by the memory of Luke as a wolf running so easily through the woods.

They made their way back to their dorm room, Izzie opening the tall wooden door. She stopped, listening to the exchange of howls in the distance.

There were still three hours left until they had to be downstairs, so Izzie curled up on her bed, staring out the window at the last bit of darkness. She could still see the bright amber glow of Luke's eyes and feel the beating of her heart in her chest. She cared deeply about a shifter; a wolf. It was hard to take it in.

6

The morning bell rang loudly, and their breakfast plates disappeared in a flash. Emma frowned, took her last bite of watermelon, and set down her fork. The group stood up quietly; Izzie was still in a haze, Alison's mind was on Tanner, and the rest of them not fully awake yet.

Alison gathered her books and the others did the same before heading for class.

"Go ahead. I'll catch up," said Alison. "I want to find Tanner and say hello. He came in late, and just sat at a random table and scarfed down food."

Izzie sighed and shook her head. "Boys! I get it. All right, see you in class."

Izzie, Kathleen, and Peter walked out the door, Kathleen still jabbering about a hole she'd torn in her favorite pairs of tights.

"Hey, look!" Peter said, pointing at the bulletin board just outside the entrance to the great hall the students affectionately called "the cafeteria." Kathleen looked up, and a huge smile came over her face.

"Yes, yes, yes, the clubs and sports sign-ups are up. Finally! This year we can join."

They ran over and joined the crowd of older kids already huddled around the board. There were many different choices, and it was overwhelming for Izzie and the rest. There was band, the school play, sports of all kinds, special clubs, and the newspaper, which had about ten different departments.

The older students were smart, using their wands to sign up from the back so they didn't have to fight for a spot or a pen. Luke pushed through the crowd and stood in front of the Louper sign-up sheet. He had waited an entire year to be able to try out for the team, and he wasn't going to miss his chance. As he raised his pen Henry and Wyatt elbowed their way in, knocked Luke out of the way, and signed their names first.

They put their arms up, and everyone cheered as they headed to class. Izzie looked at Luke and smiled, shrugging. He scoffed and rolled his eyes, signing his name below theirs.

"What is 'Louper?'" Izzie asked.

Luke looked at her like she was crazy. "Everyone knows what Louper is."

"Obviously *not* everyone."

"It's this weird game that should really be for the nerdiest of the nerds, but it somehow turned into a jock game," Kathleen grumbled.

Luke ignored her, still not looking directly at Izzie. "It's a cool sport and a virtual reality game. You get to be a different kind of magical being and use your powers to compete against others. It's just as much a brain as a brawn game. There're too many rules to explain the whole thing," he said, looking over her head at the crowd of students behind her, "but trust me, it's fun. I've been practicing for this chance since I was in middle school."

"Wow! Well, good luck." She reached out to take his hand, but he was already pushing his way through the crowd.

"Thanks," Luke said over his shoulder, looking distracted as he walked away.

"I wanted to…"

Luke looked back and saw Izzie wrinkling her forehead, hoping for some sort of explanation for the night before, but he didn't say a thing. He shrugged and let the crowd surge in front of him.

Izzie gave up, disappointed. "Boys are exhausting." She turned back to the signup sheets. "Has to be something here for me."

Just then the sea of students parted and Scarlett walked through, strutting her stuff. Her purple hair was pulled back into two low ponytails, and she wore striped socks that came above her knees. Her Mary Janes had three-inch heels, and her dark green skirt was hiked up almost too high.

She stopped halfway through the crowd and whipped out her wand, signing her name on the list for the school production of *The Wizard of Oz*. She looked at her sidekick, Claire, and curled her bright red lip.

"The library gnomes are going to play the munchkins. It'll be hilarious. I'm sure I'll be picked for Dorothy."

Alison raised an eyebrow as she walked past Scarlet and found Izzie staring at the board. "What is everyone doing?"

"The signups are out for the different clubs and events for the entire year. There's the school play, the talent show, the Young Entrepreneurs Club, Louper, ROTC, and a hundred other things. Is there anything you are interested in?"

Alison thought for a moment. "Actually, yeah. Put me down on the Talent Show."

Emma's surprised look matched Izzie's. "Oh, okay. I mean, sure."

"Why do you sound surprised?" Alison laughed.

"I'm not. Well, yeah, I am, but it's cool, I'm excited to see you perform your...talent." Izzie laughed as she put Alison's name down on the list.

Peter stood next to David, one of the older students, who was staring at the different lists. David was smart, but popular at the same time. He was known for always wearing his flat-billed baseball cap and having shaggy hair. Everyone saw him as a slacker and underestimated his magical ability—just the way he liked it.

But he had more than one talent to his name. He wrote his name down for lighting crew for the school play. "You should join us. I've heard about what you've been doing in spells class with your science hacks." He handed the pen to Peter, who smiled and wrote his name underneath.

David pointed at him with a wink and walked off as Peter also put his name down for the school newspaper.

"A scholar and a storyteller. You're gonna make us all look bad." Ethan slapped him on the back, grinning. "You should write a column about all of your magical Franken-stein tech failures. It would be hilarious."

"Hardy har. How about I do an expose on your next April Fool's joke? There's a lot going on in this school."

"Like the toombie," said Ethan, nodding at Tanner on the far side of the crowd.

"Leave him alone. He got used. The real story is who used him. No one seems to know."

"You're gonna save the world, Peter…maybe. I have better things to do."

"Like get yourself in trouble just to make people laugh?"

"You *do* get me!"

Izzie held the end of the pen in her mouth and stared at the tryouts for the *Wizard of Oz*. She had thought about acting for as long as she could remember; even had a memory of putting on shows when she was little to whom she assumed were the other kids in the orphanage. This was her chance, but she knew she was going to piss some people off. She shrugged and wrote her name on the audition list, capped the pen and turned around.

Claire glared, looking her up and down. The crowd grew quiet, waiting to see what would happen next. But, after a few very awkward moments, Claire shrugged and laughed.

"Well, *someone* has to play the witch."

Kathleen whispered under breath, "*You* already have that one down."

The others snickered as Claire whipped around, rolled her eyes, and flipped one of her braids. Alison put her hand in the air and Kathleen gave her a high five. Izzie just laughed, hooked her arm in Alison's, and sighed.

"Come on, let's get to class before we get mowed down by the Hollywood glam squad."

"Those heels would hurt." Kathleen grimaced.

Ethan and Emma stood at the board and stared at the same paper. David walked back to put his name under the Entrepreneurs Club. This was the perfect place for Ethan. It was where magic mixed with technology to come up with new inventions to change the world, or in Ethan's case, make someone a whole lot of money. Peter was in it for the creativity, and because Emma was interested. Emma wanted to help the world, but Ethan—all he could see were dollar signs.

He was second in line, too busy joking around with Peter to notice who was in front of him. When she turned around and he realized it was Grace, he froze. She noticed his demeanor and giggled, handing him the pen.

"Good choice in clubs. We'll have fun." She smiled.

All Ethan could do was shake his head and try to keep his jaw shut. Peter elbowed him in the ribs as he stared at Grace walking off. He shook his head and signed his name and then Peter's, and handed the pen to Emma. She giggled at the frozen zombie look on his face and scribbled her name down.

"Why don't you talk to her? And I mean *talk*, not scream." Emma giggled.

"I tried that. Even had a dance with her last year, but I still can't get past it. She is the girl everyone wants to date, and besides, she is super-smart."

"So?" Emma furrowed her brow.

"So, she will hang out with me for an hour and realize

how stupid I am. That will be the end of something that never began."

"You don't give yourself enough credit. Besides, it's high school. No one dates you for your brains."

"Hmm, good point." Ethan nodded.

Peter narrowed his eyes and put up his finger, but decided not to say anything. Ethan put his arm around him and ruffled his hair, knowing that statement definitely had thrown him for a loop.

"It's okay buddy. We'll explain it all when you're older."

They laughed and headed off to class. To the right of the main bulletin board was another one, full of the clubs people hoped would become popular, although most ended up with a couple of members at most. Standing around that board was a group of young wizards and witches who had modified their school uniforms to look like suits.

The girls wore their hair pulled back tight at their necks, and all the boys sported a raised eyebrow like they were constantly deep in thought. One by one they signed their names to the sheet for the Future Leaders' Club. Really what that meant was they would end up becoming politicians, business owners, or trust-fund babies.

They liked to talk because they liked the sound of their own voices, and a debate was always a bust because everyone thought the exact same way about just about everything.

This group didn't even need a club since they were together all the time, but they were obsessed with college résumés and figured it would help them get into their Ivy League colleges if they had a bunch of extracurriculars on them. None of who they called "The Outsiders" would even think about signing up for the club, nor would they be welcomed.

Next to them on a lonely board by itself was the sign-up sheet for the magical government's version of the ROTC, Reserve Officer Training Corps. It was General Anderson's addition, and his greatest hope was that the school would fulfill its mission to provide a pipeline of magical students trained to work in various branches of the government.

Only one kid stood in front of the sheet, looking right and left and trying to hide his face. He had been told by his parents that he should sign up, especially since his dad worked for the Magical Division.

"Not into being an outcast, Dad," he muttered. He hemmed and hawed, lifted his pen, then lowered it. Finally, the second bell rang, sending a shiver through him, and he shook his head, walking away. "I want to be on the news-paper. Dad will just have to get used to it."

That was it—a high school like any other—and it was about to get fun.

7

It was the first class of their sophomore year, and Ethan squeaked in just as the last bell rang. Izzie sat on the right side of the second row, with Alison behind her. Tanner sat in the center of the last row with his head down, trying to avoid the irritated stares. Everyone had pegged him as a toombie and whispered about him hexing kids and casting dark magic.

Alison was his only real friend.

Professor Xander Powell stood at the front of the classroom in his dark-teal suit, pressed white shirt, and thin purple tie. His salt-and-pepper hair was pushed back but not gelled, so it was slightly poufy and stuck out here and there. Despite that, though, he was a good-looking middle-aged man, and not at all what everyone expected as their Dark Magic Professor. His rimless glasses perched high on the bridge of his nose, and he leaned back against his desk, one ankle crossed over the other, flipping through the pages of his text.

When the class finally quieted he glanced up, shut his book loudly, and pulled out his wand. Everyone's eyes went wide, and several of them laughed as he whipped around and wrote on the board behind him with magic. His handwriting was impeccable, and his name sprawled out at the top of the board in calligraphy.

Everyone opened their fresh new notebooks and started writing whatever popped up on the board. They weren't entirely sure they needed to, but since he wrote the word RULES in big bold letters, they figured he was really serious about it.

Alison stared at the professor's soul glowing brightly at the front of the class.

She could tell he was weathered and tired and had been through a lot in his life, but there wasn't a smidgen of dark magic in him, which she found odd for the teacher charged with instructing them in the subject. She figured it was probably too dangerous to have someone who actually practiced dark magic teach at the school. She really hadn't expected to learn it, just learn *about* it—not that she didn't know enough already.

He cleared his throat, and turned around to address the class.

"Welcome to my class. I am Professor Powell, and I will be your Dark Magic teacher for the semester. Listen up!" he snapped in a voice that sounded like a rumbling train. "I will now impart various required notices and wisdom from my years in this position." He pointed his wand at a cluster of boys comparing Louper scores from their favorite teams. They sheepishly sat back in their seats and settled down.

"First, let's be clear that this class was put in place to teach you how to recognize dark magic, how to avoid dark magic, and most importantly, how to counteract dark magic if you are unlucky enough to be on the receiving end of a spell. This class is *not* intended to teach you how to use dark magic, get ahead in the world of dark magic, or how to find out who uses dark magic."

He glanced at the students as he walked around the classroom, sizing them up as they shifted uncomfortably under his gaze. "I will not give you dark spells, show you how to cast dark spells, allow you to look at restricted books on dark spells, or show you examples of dark magic. Counteract spells will be used against very dangerous spells. Pay attention at all times."

He stopped in front of a young wizard who had nodded off and rapped the young man's hand with his wand, snapping him awake. "I do not wish to hear about your Great Uncle Bart who was a dark wizard, and you cannot frighten me into giving you any more information than what I teach in this class." He tapped his wand on the palm of his hand.

"You may see the headmistress or government representatives on occasion." He leaned forward, arching an eyebrow. "This is a very serious subject." A ripple of giggles went through the room. He raised his wand, sending a current of electricity that crackled and snapped across the ceiling. It got their attention.

"There are always a few who choose to ignore my wisdom and not pay very close attention in this class." He paused for effect. "It has never gone well."

There were so many faces staring up at him, and

though they all appeared to be listening, he knew that not everyone was.

"After the recent events in our school's history..." He looked directly at Tanner, who blushed as a few of the boys snickered, "you will want to pay close attention. The information you will learn will not only prepare you for when you get out of high school, but it will help you if you should find yourself in a situation like the young man still being nursed back to health. We hope that this attack will be the only one, but since we have yet to find all the culprits, we can only assume that being able to defend yourself will prove useful."

Several of the students in the front row looked back at Tanner, snickering to each other. "He's probably making a toombie list right now. They should probably not let him take the class. He will find out all our secrets."

The boys chuckled and turned back to the front. Tanner balled up his fist and ground his teeth, wanting to pounce on those kids. Alison sensed his soul, pained that he was so upset by what the others were saying. Tanner was a good guy, and she knew he'd had nothing to do with last year, but he couldn't escape the ridicule.

She wanted to cast something to teach the boys a lesson, but her magic was growing stronger every day. She was worried it would backfire on her, and in the middle of a class that was supposed to be teaching her not to mess around.

Izzie, on the other hand, had no problem putting those assholes in their place. She dropped her hand to her side and pulled in a thin stream of energy. She twisted her hand and shot out a pea-sized fireball that split into three smaller balls behind the boys, then slid under the seats of their pants. Alison felt the energy and pressed her fingers to her mouth to stifle a laugh.

Izzie shook the magic from her hand, blinking her eyes till they stopped glowing, and looked down at the book in front of her. Suddenly one of the three boys yelled and jumped from his seat, patting the butt of his pants as smoke wafted around him.

Professor Powell lifted an eyebrow and looked at the other two, who held tightly to their desks, trying not to jump up too. They grimaced, and sweat poured down their forehead. The magic had given all three boys a hot seat. Alison covered her mouth and stifled a giggle as everyone else laughed.

Professor Powell waved his wand to cool down the seats, and the two boys let out a sigh of relief and leaned back. Alison looked back, sensing the change in Tanner's soul as he stifled a laugh and nodded gratefully at Izzie. Izzie smirked and faced front, narrowing her eyes at the boy who was taking his seat again.

She wasn't about to let her best friend's boyfriend—or whatever he was—be ridiculed in class. If nothing else, she knew how it felt to be alone and to have everyone look at you like you had two heads. If Alison loved him and trusted him, then she would too, and she would defend all three of them from the assholes around them.

"All right, if we have settled the score, let's move on to our first lesson. We're going to practice a spell that is meant to reverse any spell that harms someone else on a very minor level. I need a volunteer."

No one raised their hand. Professor Powell searched

the crowd, his eyes falling on Ethan. "Ethan, since you were the last one to show up today, you can be my example. Come up to the front."

Ethan grumbled and zipped up his hoodie as he shuffled to the front of the class. Professor Powell whispered something to him and flicked his wand. Ethan looked around, then lifted his arms to make sure he still had all his limbs, his skin wasn't purple, and he wasn't floating off the ground. Nothing. No changes.

"Ethan, repeat the alphabet for me."

Ethan shrugged and started talking. "A, Bbbb, Cccc, D, E, PhphphF...."

His eyes grew wide, and he shut his mouth as the professor slowly smiled. "Not to worry. It's not permanent, but several students are going to attempt a reversal spell on you."

Peter's hand immediately shot up in the air. Professor Powell pointed at him. "Come on up, Peter. I've heard you have a proclivity with technical magic. Why don't you add in an element of that to your spell?"

Ethan's eyes grew wide again, and he stared at the professor in fear. "Part of the lesson, Ethan. Stand still. Go ahead, Peter."

Peter nodded and walked up with a bottle of water in his hand. He took off the lid and waved his wand, pulling several drops from the bottle, and floated them in front of Ethan's face. He swirled his wand, letting a shimmering gold magic wrap around the droplets and surge through them. When the magic dissipated, the drops glimmered with gold flecks.

"All right, Ethan, tilt your head back and open up."

"Nnnnnope," he stuttered.

"Do as you're told," Professor Powell ordered firmly. "There is nothing in there that will kill you. They made me promise that wouldn't happen." He gave a crooked smile that didn't do much to comfort Ethan, but he started to do it anyway.

Ethan closed his eyes and sighed. "You're not getting out of it," Peter whispered. "Give me a chance. I think I've got this." Ethan looked at him, startled, doing his best to pantomime, *you think?* He tilted his head back and opened his mouth, letting Peter drip the glimmering water down his throat. He closed his mouth and swallowed, then opened one eye and looked around nervously.

"All right, say your alphabet again, please."

"A, B, C, D, E... Hey, it worked, and it even tasted like cinnamon. *Nice.*"

Professor Powell clapped his hands. "Very good work, Peter. I am very impressed. Why the water and gold?"

"The normal spell tends to upset stomachs, and can cause momentary blackouts and other adverse effects. By adding a material that is not foreign with a calming tone of cinnamon, the body is more receptive to it."

"Very clever." Professor Powell nodded. "I am impressed. Thank you, boys. You can take your seats. Class, I'm not suggesting you just start mixing spells if you don't know what you are doing, but can you see that not everything is written in stone? We can help others in need by using our natural talents."

8

Izzie sat on the end of her bed, reading the script for the *Wizard of Oz*. She had been studying it since she signed up, and really hoped she didn't forget any of the lines. She wanted to make a good impression and prayed she wouldn't end up as one of the flying monkeys or a random tree. She hummed the tune of *Somewhere Over the Rainbow* as she flipped from page to page.

Emma walked into the room and flung her bookbag on her bed, then took off her school robes and pulled on a sweater since she felt the chill of the seasons changing. She walked happily over to Izzie and tapped her on the knee. Izzie marked her place with her finger and looked up curiously.

"Tryouts start in like ten minutes, and I figured I'd go with you for moral support. You know, since you are going up against the actual Wicked Witch for the part of Dorothy?"

Izzie sighed in relief. "That'd be awesome. I was nervous about going on my own. Thank you."

"Sure." Emma smiled. "But we better get on it. We don't want to be late and end up a flying monkey or something."

"Tell me about it." Izzie rolled her eyes. "I'll probably end up one anyway."

Emma pointed at her. "There will be none of that. All confidence walking into this thing. You can't get what you want if you don't envision it, right?"

"I guess." Izzie giggled. "When did you get so motivating and positive?"

Emma opened the door and walked out, with Izzie behind her. "I don't know. After last year, I told myself, 'This is the year. This is when I will come into my own.' I don't want to tag along behind a Kathleen for the rest of my life. I want to be a leader in my world."

"You are doing a fantastic job of it already." Izzie giggled.

The girls walked down the hall toward the auditorium and paused, looking into the room where the Entrepreneurs Club was meeting. Peter, Ethan, Grace, and David stood around a table, fanning small green flames that rose from whatever they were working on. Grace raised her wand and shot out a stream of light, extinguishing the flames. A plume of smoke radiated up from a collection of burnt wires.

Everyone fanned the air, coughing, and Emma scrunched her nose. The smoke made everything smell like swamp water. Izzie looked at Emma and back at them.

"I thought you signed up for that?"

"I did, but I'm not sure if it's for me. As you can see, it's a bit more than just hoping for a better tomorrow, and I don't know if I want to mix my magic with Ethan's."

"I'm not sure I would either." Izzie giggled.

———

At the end of the hall behind closed doors, the Future Leaders' Club held its first session. They had already elected a president, secretary, and treasurer, and all sat quietly in their business suits looking up at the front. They did everything by the book. If anyone tried a shortcut, they were called out immediately. The president banged his gavel on the desk and looked at the others.

"We are calling into session our very first meeting of the Future Leaders' Club. Our secretary is taking minutes, but I suggest everyone else keep their own clear and concise notes. Normally we'd start the meeting with a review of the last meeting's minutes, but since this is our first one of the year, we will begin with a run-through of the rules."

Everyone nodded their heads and jotted notes in their leather-covered binders. They were in a very serious mood, and they resembled droids, all sitting in the exact same way. The boys sat up straight in their chairs, and the girls did as well, but with their feet crossed at the ankles. Most of them had business cards on the desks in front of them, and fancy pens in their hands. Since they didn't know whether they would be working in the magical world or the normal world, it was a rule that all notes were handwritten and magic was used only on very special occasions.

"You are to show up on time, if not early to every meeting. Remember, fifteen minutes early is on time, and on time is late in the business world. You will take all notes by hand. You will wait until the speaker has finished to ask questions, and you will remain professional at all times, even during debates. We all know what happened last year when Rupert spoke against an idea when it wasn't his turn. We'll just say his tie was crooked last time I saw him."

Everyone chuckled for just a moment and went back to writing. "Now, we are going to start this year off with a bang and have a debate. The right side of the room will be on one side, the left on the other. We will be discussing the rise of magic in the world, and the role magical beings should be playing in the government. Now, I know we all agree on this subject, but it wouldn't be a debate if we didn't have opposing views, so I pick the right side to argue *against* the role of magical beings in the government."

Everyone on the right side pouted slightly, and the president chuckled. "Now, now, we can't always be on the winning side, especially when we are working alongside the normies, you know…the humans. All right, teams, assemble!"

Izzie and Emma walked by and looked in the window. "I finally get what they mean about watching paint dry. That would be more entertaining."

Emma giggled as they entered the auditorium.

Izzie and Emma took a seat in the third row, trying to ignore Claire's angry stares. Lucy Fowler stood on the stage going through stacks of papers, dressed in a hand-knitted vest with the words Theatre Is the Heart of the Soul embroidered lopsided on the back. Her crazy red hair was down and sticking out all over the place, smashed down on top by a bright red beret. She passed down hand-outs with sidebars for the different roles, and they handed them back row by row until they reached Izzie and Emma.

Izzie looked back at the last row of seats and Horace smiled, giving her a thumbs-up. She returned a nervous smile and turned back around. Professor Fowler took in a dramatic deep breath. She put her hands out to each side and swished her wild hair around.

"Theatre... It is the essence of humanity, and we here at the School of Necessary Magic have a knack for the theatrics of it all. Combining raw talent and a little bit of magic, we put on shows you will be proud of. Now, raise your hand if you are auditioning for the coveted role of Dorothy."

Only Claire and Izzie's hands went up. Claire looked back at the hushed murmur, surprised to see Izzie's raised hand. She'd thought she made sure that no one but her auditioned, but she wasn't worried. She had been in every play since her sophomore year. Professor Fowler ignored the tension in the seats and took her place at the table at the side of the stage.

Izzie and Emma watched as several people with varying skill levels got up and sang, danced, and read lines in strange voices to try to land the parts they were auditioning for. Some of them were good. Others made everyone want to crawl under their seats. None of the freshmen were allowed to audition for the main roles, since they'd only been added when it was realized there weren't enough signups to fill the parts. They were given the roles of flying monkeys, which eased Izzie's mind because she really didn't want to be cast as one.

"Claire, you're next," Professor Fowler announced.

Claire cleared her throat and climbed up on the stage, holding her hands in front of her. She read through the part in an exaggerated and overly-dramatic manner, then bowed to the applause of her friends in the front row. At the end, she sang *Over the Rainbow*. Everyone plastered on a smile, even though her voice cracked and shimmied through the whole thing.

"Holy lord, she sounds like a dying cat," Emma whispered, sinking down in her chair.

"Thank you, Claire." Professor Fowler smiled forcefully. "You may take your seat. Izzie, you're next."

Izzie took a deep breath and nodded at Emma, who smiled and patted her on the leg. She walked up to the stage, ignoring the whispers from the front row, and took her place center stage. As she began the crowd quieted, watching her put everything she had into the part. She was a very believable Dorothy, and even Emma was impressed. Professor Fowler ran her through an extra few lines, pissing Claire off no end.

When she was done, the music started, cueing her to sing *Over the Rainbow*. Emma held her breath, hoping she was at least better than Claire. As soon as Izzie's soft, flowing voice hit her ears, she sighed in relief. Professor Fowler clutched her clipboard to her chest, listening intently to every note. Claire leaned over, talking loudly to her friends.

"Too bad she's an orphan. Even if she did get the part, no one would be there to watch her."

The girls laughed. Izzie tried her best to ignore her, but she started to get angry. "Look, she knows she is wasting her time. She doesn't even look like Dorothy. More like a scarecrow."

Izzie closed her eyes and continued to sing, not realizing her magic was building inside her. Horace sat forward in his seat when he noticed the bright glow that moved up from her feet and gathered at her chest. The more Claire picked at her, the brighter the light got, until you could barely see her on the stage. Emma covered her eyes, knowing it was bad. Horace jumped up and ran for the stage. When he reached the edge he reached up to ground her, but it was too late. She belted out the last note and her magic exploded, sending a surge of energy outward to whomp everyone in its path.

The students were forced back against the backs of their chairs and Horace was knocked from his feet and down the aisle. Emma covered her mouth and ran for the stage. Slowly Izzie opened her eyes, already knowing what had happened. She'd felt the pressure in her chest, but by that point it was too late. All she had heard was Claire's shrill laughter, which fed her emotions, which fueled her magic. It was like the darkness in Claire pulled at the light inside her, something she had never felt before.

She looked around as everyone sat there staring wide-eyed at her, then jumped down and raced to Horace's side. She bent down with a sad look on her face, and he groaned as he sat up and patted her on the shoulder.

"That was a powerful song there." He chuckled.

"Sorry."

9

————————

Between study hall and the next class, Izzie snuck away from the others to have a moment to herself. She was still shaken that she'd blasted the entire auditorium with a surge of energy she hadn't seen coming until it was too late. She'd worked all summer get her magic under control, and thought she had. Instead, she had allowed a girl to get to her with cruel words, then bam—she knocked her friend to the ground. She was just glad she'd let it go when she had, or she might have blown the whole room up.

She walked over to the door that led out to the small garden at the side of the school. As she reached for the door her hand grazed another and she pulled back, looking up to see Luke. He was startled, obviously caught up in his own thoughts.

"Oh, sorry. I'll just..." He turned to walk away, but Izzie grabbed his hand.

Go bold or go home, Izzie told herself before she swung

open the garden door and pulled Luke in. They were the only two out there, and Luke looked almost shy, standing there with her. She jumped in straight away.

"You didn't scare me at all. I mean," she hesitated, "as a wolf. I don't look down on you because you're a wolf. People think *I'm* a hidden toombie, after all." She wrinkled her nose, trying to get him to smile. "Everyone is afraid I'm going to go off at any moment, and it doesn't help that I blasted the auditorium with energy at my audition. Half the kids were terrified, and the others impressed."

"I heard about that." He chuckled. "I'm sorry it happened. Emma said Claire was saying some really nasty things, and she was about to zap her when you pretty much took care of it."

"I'm not a toombie. I'm just not in full control of my magic, that's all." She sighed, sitting down on one of the stone benches.

Luke's face sank, having not meant to offend her. "That's not what I meant. I just meant, well, she deserved it, and nobody got hurt, so it's okay. I think I know by now that you don't have a dark spot in your whole body."

"Thanks." Izzie chuckled. "And I know that shifters are part of our community and that you are pretty awesome at it. I was surprised to see you, that's all. If I looked scared, that wasn't what I was feeling. I just didn't expect to see a wolf come out of the bushes, or me be able to touch your fur, which I have to add is super-soft. I don't know why I expected differently, but it was awesome."

"It's the Pantene," he joked.

They both laughed and looked down at their feet. Luke sighed and rubbed his hand through his hair.

"It's weird. Like I'm this wolf, and I have learned how to control that most of the time. I mean, that's the first thing they taught me. But I feel like I'm constantly learning new things about my power, like telepathy with other wolves, or super strength. Those things just keep like being sprung on me. I feel like I'm on the f—"

"The fringe?" Izzie laughed. "Yeah, I totally get that. The thing is, There's no one I can talk to except Alison. I don't know who my parents were. The only thing I've ever been told is I am a Light Elf, but until I got here, I didn't even know what that meant. I don't even know if I'm a normal elf. All the elves I know describe their magic in a totally different way than mine is, and it just keeps getting stronger."

"That has to be tough, not having your own people to talk to. I never thought you were a toombie, but I've seen your magic in action, and you seem a lot stronger than a normal Light Elf. But then again, I don't know a lot about it, or even know what that feels like."

Footsteps caught Izzie's and Luke's attention. Claire and her posse walked through the garden toward the doors. She looked at Izzie and paused for a moment before giving her a nod of respect. Izzie was taken completely off-guard, not having expected that reaction. She glanced at Luke, who looked just as shocked, and watched as Claire flung open the door, barking orders at her group.

"Ice cream, stat, and damn it, can you not put the gummy bears on there this time like complete morons? They turn into little rocks."

Izzie shook her head and rubbed her temples, feeling like she had fallen into some sort of alternate universe. She couldn't figure out which way was up anymore. First, Claire wanted to take her out, and now that she had blasted her with a raging beam of energy, she gave her a nod of respect. She was starting to think she had no idea how the whole social construct of magical beings really worked.

"*That* was weird." Luke chuckled.

"Uh, yeah. I mean, I'll take it over being made fun of or beat up, but now my head is completely screwed up."

"She does have a point. Gummy bears turn into little cement blocks when you put them on ice cream."

"I know, right? Who does that? Marshmallows too. You think it's going to be delicious, but they get hard and chewy and stick in your teeth."

"Hot fudge, sprinkles, maybe caramel, and I'm good."

"Don't forget whipped cream," Izzie pointed out.

They chuckled for a moment. Luke stretched his arms up over his head. "The truth is, I slip out sometimes to run with a local pack that my family set me up with. We have to be really careful not to be seen by the local humans, and even the magical community around here doesn't like it too much. They aren't shifter people, I can tell, but then again, who is? Not to mention that the dark families are always looking for us. They are constantly trying to hurt us, or at least mess with us. In wolf form we can fight back pretty well, but if they catch a newbie or someone changing back... Well, we don't have a chance against magic."

"Are there wolves out here? Like, not shifters, but wolves from the wild?"

"No, not that I know of, which is why we have to make

sure not to be seen by humans. That would create an entirely different set of problems, and it's dangerous. Humans tend to pull out shotguns when wolves are around, and even as shifters we don't fare well under fire."

"No, I suppose none of us really do when it comes to being shot at. Thanks for talking to me about it, though. I was worried you would think I was upset since I know how others talk about shifters. But I wasn't. I thought it was really cool."

Luke smiled and bumped her with his shoulder. "You should see us when it's a full moon. It's wild out there."

"I bet." Izzie chuckled.

Just then the bell rang inside, and they both got up and pulled on their bookbags. They were headed to the same class, but Izzie wished they had more time to talk. She was glad they got to talk at all, though, since she'd started to think Luke was going to spend the rest of the semester dodging her.

Luke held the door open for Izzie and stepped faster to catch up with her. They walked in comfortable silence down the hall, watching as Ethan bolted from the other direction to try to beat the tardy bell. Izzie laughed and stepped to the side of the door, letting Ethan run through huffing and puffing. Luke shook his head and rolled his eyes as he walked in behind them. They took seats next to each other at the back of the class, smiled shyly, and pulled out their books.

It felt good to both of them talk to someone who understood what they were going through, maybe not on a specific basis, but definitely in a roundabout way. Izzie had Alison, but Luke really didn't have anyone. The older shifters ignored him, and most of the other kids in class already had their packs. He remembered that night and wasn't sure if he should even have stepped out of the bushes, but with Izzie's reaction and now verbal confirmation, he was really glad he had.

"Ahhh, channeling energy," Max Regency said, stepping down off his step stool. "It is the essence of every kind of magic out there, including those shifters who walk in the shadows of the magical community. People think that channeling is only for those who can do magic, like elves and witches, but surprisingly, it is for all magical beings. In this class, I am going to teach you how to use that energy to empower whatever talent you have inside you."

Emma laughed as the short Max lifted his arms in the air with gusto. He was an interesting gnome; serious most days, with an obvious love of teaching. "These are tools you will all use over and over." He stepped back up on the stool and put out his hands.

"Now, I would like the shifters in the back, the wands to the right, and the pointy ears to the left."

Everyone scurried to their spots. Those with double heritage in wizardry and elves just picked the side with most of their friends. For a moment Alison wasn't sure where she should go, but considering she performed her magic more like an elf, she headed over with Izzie. They all laughed and huddled together, waiting for further instructions.

"You can channel energy in two ways, really. By holding

hands and concentrating, or by combining your magic streams. For elves, it usually works better if you hold hands, touch wands, or just mix the stream, and shifters...."

He clapped his hands and laughed.

"Shifters, this is my favorite. By pressing your forehead once against that of another shifter who is outside your pack in your human form, you form a bond of sorts. You will be able to communicate easier telepathically, and if you stand together touching fingertips, you will be able to track others. Of course, you can already do this in wolf form, but this is without any kind of change."

Immediately the shifters huddled together, talking excitedly. The elves lined up facing the left wall, where several balloons hung. The witches and wizards did the same. They were supposed to pick a partner and combine their energy to lift a balloon as high as they could. Normally this would be simple, but since it was their first time channeling with a partner many people struggled to combine the energies and lift at the same time.

Alison grabbed Izzie's hand and looked at her soul. "You ready?"

"Always. Let's show 'em what we got."

The girls closed their eyes and latched hands tightly. It took them no time at all. As soon as the first drop of energy swirled between their clasped hands, the balloon shot to the ceiling and burst. They opened their eyes as Max walked over.

"Well, it looks like you two have more than a connection." He chuckled.

10

One of the main courses taught from the second year on, the very foundation of the School of Necessary Magic, was *Integration with Normals*. This was a class that every semester included different outings with the non-magicals. It started small during the sophomore year and grew over the remaining two years of the student's high school career. The magical parents and teachers weren't all that fond of the class, claiming it taught the kids to hide who they really were, but those who lived, functioned, and mixed with the normals knew that it was essential to maintaining the rules set forth by the governing bodies.

Although many knew about magic, and the world of Oriceran, It was considered inappropriate to use magic in front of the non-magical.

This class was very important, and a cornerstone for graduation from the school. It had been the main mission of the founders and backers of the school, the United States Government. Almost all magical schools around the world, seeing the benefits of the education, had adopted the courses in one way or another, and Mara Berens was in charge of it. It was far too important to be left to anyone else.

That morning Mara paced her office, trying to remember every last detail of the day's plans. It was to be a simple day, but that didn't make her any less nervous about it. Over her years as headmistress she'd only had one bad moment during these lessons, but it had been necessary to save the humans involved and had not reflected on the student's ability to mix in. Dark families had arrived at a time when light magic was battling for control over the dark. It still haunted her every time she thought about it. With the chaos in town and the arrival of the dark wizards, she'd thought about canceling it altogether, but her superiors wouldn't hear of it. They'd told her it was even *more* essential now, and that her duty was to make sure the students grew to be happy, healthy, and law-abiding magical citizens.

Mara was a bit irritated by that, but she hid it behind a happy face and carried out her duties. If an outing were to happen, she would make sure it was safe, short, and to the point. She grabbed her purse and headed to the auditorium where the sophomores quietly waited for her. As she entered the whispers settled and she stood on the stage to address them.

"Sophomores, thank you for your quiet attention today. This is an exciting day. We will be practicing integrations with normals. As you know, this is an extremely important event and will count highly toward your graduation in three years. Even if you pass every class with flying colors, you will be held back until you pass this one. Now, I have arranged a very simple mixer for your first attempt. We will be meeting with other kids your age from a nearby private school, Charlottesville Preparatory. The meet and greet will take place at one of the small restaurants in town for lunch. You may not give away that you know magic. Now, on the surface, it sounds easy, but you have to consider what these kids will ask you. Everyone is curious about this school, and they might want to know what classes you take. I have instructed Mr. Rigby to hand out little sheets to everyone with the lists of normals' version of sophomore class schedules. If someone asks you, those are the classes you are taking. And please try to memorize it since it looks a bit suspicious if you have to read it off a paper to them."

Mara shook her head, slightly exasperated that she had to explain the little things. She had, however, learned that lesson early on. She'd given past classes way too much credit for thinking about the small details and ended up with a huge mess to clean up and a whole bunch of human memories to erase. Suffice it to say; the government had not been happy with her.

"Now, I will be there if you have questions, as will Professor Hudson and Horace, so find us at any time. If everything goes well, I have a special treat for you all afterward. Follow the professors single-file out to the bus, and please try to keep the voices low. Classes are still in session."

Mara watched with concern as the students excitedly filed out of the auditorium. She knew that most of them had some, if not tons, of experience blending with normies from before they attended the school. The funny thing about magical beings—especially teenagers—was that when they started to live in a magical world, they seemed to forget how to integrate into normal life. Luckily the headmistress of the prep school was a close friend of hers and a Light Elf, so if anything went wrong, she would be able to assist with the cleanup.

The bus was packed, and the students' conversations were excited and loud. Alison and Tanner sat at the back across from Izzie and Luke. Ethan and Peter were in the seat in front of them, and to the other side Aya, Emma, and Kathleen squeezed into another one. Ethan looked over the back of his seat at Luke.

"Hey, if all hell breaks loose, just turn into your wolf and let them pet your belly. That should do it."

Luke balled up his list and threw it at Ethan's head, making a face. Izzie giggled at the two of them and watched the front as the professors boarded and took seats. Mara looked nervous, not that Izzie could blame her. *She* wouldn't want to be the one taking that group out and expecting there not to be trouble. Just Ethan alone had the potential to make a huge problem for her.

Mara nodded to the bus driver and sat down next to Horace. "What could go wrong?"

Horace raised an eyebrow and Mara shook her head, facing forward as the bus headed to the restaurant. When they arrived, everyone was on their best behavior as they filed excitedly into the restaurant and took their seats. They were mixed in with the other kids. Lunch had been selected for them, but no one really cared about the food. Mara had been nervous about her kids, but what she hadn't accounted for was the curiosity level of the prep school kids, and just how mischievous they could be for humans.

Izzie and the others had chosen to stay together, sitting at a large round table in the back corner with four of the prep school students. There were two boys and two girls, and they immediately launched into a barrage of questions, slightly disappointed and unbelieving when they got normal high school answers. As lunch progressed they started to loosen up with each other, laughing and talking about the different happenings at the prep school. One of the boys looked at the professors and saw that they were engrossed in their own conversations.

He pulled his bookbag up and whispered to the others, "Look what I got from my uncle over summer vacation."

He pulled out a small firecracker and smiled. "It's a new kind from London. You're supposed to be able to click the wick, and then you can stop it at any time before it hits the explosive. It's not even loud. It just makes a really gross-smelling fog that takes forever to get out of a building. I haven't used one yet. I just like playing with the wicks.

Izzie raised an eyebrow, feeling this was not a good idea. The boy flicked his fingers against the wick and it turned red, slowly moving toward the base. He flicked his fingers again, but nothing happened. Over and over he tried, panicking when it wouldn't turn off. Right before it hit the base, he tossed it into the center of the table.

"Oh, no! This is so bad. We'll be expelled for sure."

Ethan looked at the others, holding his wand beneath his robes. They watched as a small trickle of smoke poured out, steadily getting faster. The smell was already terrible, and they all knew that if it spread they would all be in huge trouble. Finally, Ethan shook his head and pulled out his wand, whispering a reversal spell. The normals watched with wide eyes as the light curled around the smoke and pushed it back into the firecracker. Even the wick was returned to full power.

"Whoa," the boys whispered. "I knew it! You all *are* magical, aren't you?"

"We aren't supposed to let normal people like you know," Izzie hissed. "We will all be held back if our headmistress finds out."

Ethan shoved his wand back into his sleeve. "And she'll have to wipe your memories."

The kids looked at each other, then back at Ethan and the others. "You saved our butts. We would have been toast for sure. Your secret is safe with us, we swear."

They all smiled at each other and Izzie breathed a sigh of relief, watching the boy carefully pick up the firecracker and put it back into his bookbag. By the end of the luncheon, they all felt like friends and agreed to meet up in town again some weekend during free time. Izzie walked up to Alison as they climbed back onto the buses and let out a deep breath.

"That was a close one." Alison chuckled. "I knew that boy was trouble. I could see his soul, and it was pure mischief until the firecracker went off. Then it was pure fear. I bet he peed his pants a little."

They laughed and took their seats at the back, and looked up as Mara happily climbed on board. "All right, guys. You did an amazing job; probably the best any class has done their first time out. Thank you so much for behaving and doing exactly as you should have."

Izzie glanced at Luke as he stifled a laugh. The doors to the bus shut, and Mara smiled at the students.

"As a treat for doing so well, we are going to head to downtown Charlottesville and visit the mall!"

Everyone was excited. They loved the mall area. The mall wasn't like other large complexes. It *was* downtown Charlottesville, a historic wonder and the apple of the locals' eyes. All the old buildings had been converted into stores, restaurants, and inns, but the heritage had been neatly preserved. The magical students liked it because any of the towns old statues or plaques with small stars at the bottom revealed the magical history of the town when touched by a magical being. Best of all, none of the humans could see it when it appeared, so they could literally be standing next to a normal and watch the magical history of Charlottesville without them being any the wiser.

It was a nice treat on a day that could quite easily have been a huge disaster.

11

Today was the day; the one Luke and so many others had been waiting for. It was the boys' Louper team tryouts. They all sat in the cafeteria already geared up, looking through different Louper books to make sure they were completely ready. Of course, Wayne and Henry sat cockily with the upperclassmen tossing back eggs and some bagels, but the sophomores were more than nervous. It was the first year they were permitted to try out for the team, and for some, only the third or fourth time they had played the game.

The gang was having a leisurely breakfast since it was the start of the weekend and making plans for later that day. Kathleen glanced at the door when Luke walked in wearing his favorite Louper team jersey and a pair of windbreaker pants. He clutched the Louper bible to his chest. The book contained all the rules and tricks, and a description of the best players to start as. His eyes were red and puffy, and Kathleen could tell he'd spent all night studying the thing. She'd normally give him a hard time about it, but she felt for him, especially as a shifter trying out for a team of magical beings.

"Woohoo, look at Mr. Louper coming in for the kill." Kathleen smiled.

The others looked up and gave him rousing applause, whooping and hollering and embarrassing the crap out of him. He bowed his head and grinned, his cheeks bright red. Izzie smiled at him as he sat down, and a plate of fruit popped up in front of him.

"Are you nervous?"

"A little." He chuckled. "But hopefully everything goes smoothly."

"I'll be cheering for you." She smiled.

"Thanks."

"Us too," Ethan said, yanking Peter up. "And check it out!"

He pointed at the SNM Louper logo on the front of his shirt and they both turned around, jerking their thumbs over their shoulders. Written in big bold letters across their shoulders was Team Luke "The Wolfman" Jackson. Izzie frowned, wishing she had one too.

Luke laughed. "That's really awesome. Are you trying out?"

Ethan sat down shaking his head. "Nah, but we figured we'd come sit in the stands and watch the action if old Regency lets us."

"Nice, although I don't know how much action you'll see the first day."

"We are there to support you."

At that moment, an announcement echoed across the cafeteria.

"All those signed up to try out for the Louper team, Professor Regency is ready on the Louper grounds behind the school."

Luke took another bite of his fruit and picked up his book, smiling at the others. "Well, wish me luck."

"You don't need it. You're gonna kick butt," Alison said happily.

Luke ran out of the cafeteria and through the back doors of the mansion, jogging out onto the Louper field. Everyone lined up quickly, the upperclassmen on the right and the sophomores on the left. Mr. Regency turned toward the group. He was wearing a miniature coaching jersey and held a clipboard that was half the size of his chest. A couple of the guys snickered, and Max stopped and stared at them. They were upperclassmen and had been on the team the previous year.

"I want to point out that just because you were on the team last year does not mean you automatically have the right to be on the team this year. Now, since we do everything as a team, I want everyone to drop their things and do twelve laps around the field—no magic. You can all thank Wayne and Henry, since they can't seem to handle the fact that I am short."

Everyone groaned except for Luke, who took off in the lead. Max took notice and nodded, jotting a note next to his name. He narrowed his eyes at Wayne and Henry, who tried to make a break for Luke, most likely to push him off the field or something equally juvenile. He waved his wand discreetly and shoved it in his pocket, looking up at the sky while he whistled and rocked back and forth.

Eleanor Hudson was on the side, conducting cheer tryouts for the Louper team. She looked suspiciously at Max and he tried to look innocent. Just then she heard groaning from Wayne and Henry. They slowed their pace, scratching feverishly at their crotches. She glanced again at Max, who was laughing, and gave him a stern look. He sighed and pulled out his wand, reversing the spell. She nodded and turned back toward the girls, chuckling. She knew they deserved it. They were little jerks, but she couldn't condone it in public like that.

There had been a few times when she had wanted to do the same thing and worse to students, but corporal punishment was strictly against the rules. She put her hands up to restart the routine she'd taught. She grimaced at a couple of girls, who had absolutely no rhythm and ended up ramming into each other and falling to the ground. She didn't know what it was about that school, but unlike normal high schools, there wasn't a flood of girls who wanted on the squad. She had hoped Kathleen would come out with all her dance experience, but she didn't seem even slightly interested.

The boys huffed and puffed around the long track, hitting the straightaway at the end for their final lap. Luke trotted up, barely out of breath, followed by a few upperclassmen, then Wayne and Henry, who held their sides as they huffed and puffed. Max raised an eyebrow and shook his head.

"I told you not to eat eggs and bagels before practice, boys. You never listen."

The boys coughed and hacked as they caught their breath. Wayne laid down on the ground and splashed water over his face. Max took a deep breath and walked over to the upperclassmen, counting one, two, one, two until all of them had a number. He tried to keep it simple, knowing that some of the players weren't the sharpest crayons in the box.

"All right, if you are a number one, line up on the right side of the field. If you are a number two, line up on the left. Sophomores, stay where you are. I will be back in just a minute."

The sophomore tryouts milled in a circle making small talk with each other. "Who are *we* going to play?"

"Well, we can't play the normies, and those guys would kick our asses just to laugh at us," one of the boys responded.

"Maybe we will practice on each other. You know, start out easy, and then he will keep challenging us until we fall out."

"If that's the case, there will be like two of us standing at the end," another boy said with a chuckle. "No offense, but I've been playing since I was a little kid and I couldn't take on Wayne or Henry. Their players are so strong."

Luke shook his head. "It's not about how strong *they* are. It's about how smart *you* are. I watched a Milltown Kemana game once where the newbie on the team beat the other member with a simple baseline character with no skill level. He was seriously all about showing us that it's what you do with what you have that matters."

One of the guys chuckled, patting him on the back.

"Well, seems the shifter here has an after-school lesson for us."

All the guys laughed, and Luke looked down at the ground. The guy nudged him and smiled.

"I'm just giving you a hard time. My stepdad's a shifter; best guy I know."

Luke smiled and nodded, glad that the antics hadn't started already. He never understood why he got so beat up about being a shifter, since Henry— a shifter as well—was like Mr. Popular and no one treated him different. Maybe it was his athletics that did it, which is what his dad had told him from the beginning. *Be athletic. You are stronger and keener than most because of your wolf. That will get the trolls off your back.* He didn't mean literal trolls, but Luke gave him a hard time anyway.

They looked at Max Regency as he got the upper-classmen started, then whistled to the stands. Ethan and Peter ran over with bins of equipment and not very excited looks on their faces. They stood next to Max, struggling with the bins and waiting for instructions.

"These two lovely ladies decided to show up just to watch the real men play the game, so I put them to work. I don't want you guys to get too riled up over tryouts. You are new to the high school world of sports, so I made these tryouts several weeks long. I want to see how you are from the basics on up, and see—if I put you on the team—where you will need the most work. I know you all expected to roll out here, beast up, and take down some upperclass-men, but unless you've been playing for years, that isn't going to happen. No matter what level you are in leisure, everyone starts the season at one and goes up from there, depending on moves and skill."

Max looked at Ethan and Peter and nodded. They put the bins down and handed out the equipment. Ethan walked up to Luke and nodded proudly, then beat his fist on his chest before handing him the newest piece in the box. Luke chuckled and shook his head as they gathered the bins and ran off. Max watched, blinking rapidly, and shook his head.

"Idiots," he muttered, then turned back to the group and clapped his hands. "All right, so you will be using magically-enhanced virtual reality headgear on the open field today. This is not a battle. You won't be challenging anyone, but it will give you the chance to get used to being in a virtual world and learn how to maneuver in it. This won't be as shocking to those of you who have played before but for the few where this is your first or second time, remember that you will physically be playing the game on this field with everyone else. They will be in the same world as you, only when you look around during a game, you will see them as their character. Be careful maneuvering at first. Don't get overzealous since you can be a bit wobbly your first time around. Your characters have been picked at random, and won't have any bearing on who you are if you join the team.

"Put on the headset and click the green button on the side. When you've had enough, come over and watch the upperclassmen. It's quite a show during tryouts."

Luke chuckled, knowing the boys would go all-out on the other side of the field. He was pretty sure there were more injuries during tryouts than during the playing season. He pulled his headset on and clicked the button on the side, watching the opening screen. When the field came into view, no longer just shaggy grass but perfectly trimmed AstroTurf, he held out his hands and turned them over in front of him. He chuckled. His player was an Ice Creature with large shards of ice jutting out all over his body. He watched the frost wafting from him and looked at the other guys doing the same things.

"This is gonna be good."

The year before, Mara had decimated a couple of dark wizards, sending one running back to his master to let him know the jig was up. Since then she hadn't sensed any dark magic being openly used around town, but that didn't mean it wasn't lurking in the shadows. The magical community had scouted the area as best they could, but in truth, many didn't want to get involved. They remembered the days of Rhazdon and all the deaths, and the ones who volunteered weren't well-trained in finding traces of dark magic. Mara went out all summer to help, which was why she didn't visit Leira in DC or go back to Texas to see her daughter. During the school year, though, it was a lot harder to keep track of who was coming in and out of the town.

During the day the place was full of tourists, locals, and students of the schools and the university. At night, after the bars closed, the college kids stumbled back to the dorms, and the lights went off through the town, things were a lot different. Dark forces lurked close by, shimmering through the shadows, looking for something—or maybe someone. Mara wasn't sure which but she had her suspicions, which was why she had instituted the curfew. Whatever was out there was not out for tricks and jokes. The last thing she wanted was for students out late messing around to get snatched, hexed, or worse by the dark forces at hand.

They'd had enough turmoil last semester, and their efforts to find the toombie had hit a dead end at every turn. She knew Izzie wasn't a toombie since she'd never been in an orphanage, but she couldn't tell anyone that. It was her secret, and she had promised to keep it. The only harm was that it caused the other students to have suspicions, but in a way, it shielded her from the dark forces finding out her true identity. That might be more detrimental than if she actually were the toombie.

During the weekend all the kids were excited to get away from the school for a little while, especially the group. Izzie loved Mara, but she couldn't figure out why all summer she was sooo strict about her going out. She was excited to get away from constantly being watched for a while, and with all the tryouts at school and the students going in and out of the underground kemana, Mara didn't have time to keep close tabs on Izzie.

"You ready to hit the streets?" Kathleen chuckled. She was standing in front of Izzie as she laced up her high-top Chuck Taylors.

"Yes, yes, yes." Izzie giggled. "More than ready."

"Come on, ladies. The guys are meeting us out front

with Luke. His practice is over for the day, and he definitely needs to loosen up a bit."

Izzie smiled and grabbed her purse, throwing it across her chest. She straightened her green corduroy jacket and smoothed the grey t-shirt that was loosely tucked into the front of her rolled-up jeans. Alison walked past her, and Izzie reached out, grabbing her arm and hooked hers into it. Alison flipped her hair to the side and ran her fingers through it.

"Do I look okay?"

"You look beautiful, as always," Izzie said narrowing her eyes. "Why?"

Alison shrugged. "Tanner's coming."

"Ohhhh." Izzie laughed, throwing her head back as they followed the other girls out and down the steps. "He would find you adorable if you came out in a trash-bag skirt and dish-towel top."

"I really hope that's not true." Alison laughed. "I might have to question his judgment."

They giggled as they met up with the boys and jumped on the jitney heading to town. They talked loudly in the back of the bus, listening to Luke's tales of his first day of tryouts. Izzie and Alison couldn't stop laughing when he told the story about Max, his wand, and the unfortunate sudden onset of jock itch Henry and Wyatt had had.

"Good. They deserved it," Kathleen said seriously. "Oh, it's our stop."

The bus dropped them off outside the local Starbucks. Everyone grabbed a coffee and sat down at a table near the couches. There were a couple of magical beings behind them with their backs to the students, running their mouths about dark things. Kathleen put her finger to her lips, and the group nonchalantly leaned back to listen in.

"They have it right," the guy on the right said harshly. "They need to shut down the school. It's a bloody experiment by the human government. It's another way for them to try to control the magical community and keep some of the most powerful away from our side."

"I hear you," the woman replied. "But rumors are, the dark ones aren't done trying. The first plan failed last year; that's no secret. The meddlesome headmistress and her band of goons managed to shut it down pretty fast, but this next plan, which I hear is almost fool-proof, won't fail. Before we know it, that school will be nothing but a vacant lot."

"Or the next center for the dark families." The guy laughed. "Wouldn't that be sweet justice thrown right in their faces? Always trying to keep the dark magic down and run us out of the place. If all the magicals in the area got together against the government, it would be over in a heartbeat. But the light ones gotta be the freaking heroes, getting in the way and making everything more complicated. It's really obnoxious, not to mention that we haven't had a real good up-and-coming dark one for a long time. There have been some possibilities in the past, but they always get swooped off by the light magic."

"That always seems to be the way." The woman sighed and took a swig of her coffee.

"Oh, I did hear something else," the guy said, leaning in and lowering his voice. "You know *the girl* everyone has been looking for?"

"Yeah, the one who no one in our network has been

able to find, because we aren't even sure what she looks like?"

"Yes, or who she is even supposed to be?"

"Mmmhmm. What about her?"

"Well, word is out that there is a huge reward for whoever captures her. Enough to let someone retire and disappear while the others fight the war, if you know what I mean."

Alison dropped her hands to her lap and clasped them together tightly. She wondered if the girl they were talking about was her. She knew that her biological father and the Harriken had wanted to take her out, but she didn't know if someone else had put a nationwide bounty on her head.

It wasn't like she was hiding. She'd been in Los Angeles with Shay and Brownstone all summer and had no real issues. On top of that, she was at school, and she hadn't gone to any great lengths to protect her identity.

Still, the idea frightened her a little bit, and she wondered if she should call Brownstone. She knew that if she did that, though, there was a good chance he would pull her out of school or go nuts worrying about her. She decided to wait until she had more information. She didn't want to make a fuss when it could easily be the toombie they were talking about. Everyone might suspect her of being one, but that was because most people didn't know her history.

Sure, she had technically been an orphan until Brownstone adopted her, but she hadn't spent time in an orphanage. She knew exactly where she had been and what had been done to her. She'd gone from her parents' home straight to Brownstone's. Explaining the circumstances to people without revealing her true nature, however, was a bit more complicated than she wanted to take on. *She* knew she wasn't a toombie, and she really didn't care what people thought about her. Sure, Izzie could be one, but she doubted it, and even though there was that streak of darkness in Tanner's soul, she couldn't bring herself to believe he would ever give in to it.

"All I know is that she is close by, and if I figure out who she is, you can be damn well sure I'm snatching her up in a brown satchel and dropping her right on the dark wizard's front porch, hand out and ready for my reward."

They both cackled, and Izzie shifted in her seat, looking out the window. She felt slightly dizzy, and closed her eyes for a moment to get her bearings. In her mind visions started to flash. There was a scream and a crash, then she could see herself pressed up against a brick wall, panic and sweat on her face and balls of dark magic flying past her. That was it, and none of it made any sense to her.

"You okay?" Emma asked, putting her hand on Izzie's shoulder.

Izzie jumped and gasped, shaking her head and breathing heavily. Emma furrowed her brow and handed her a napkin. Izzie blotted her forehead and looked away for a moment, gathering herself. Her heart was pounding, and she still heard the screams around her. She shook her head, trying to get rid of the dark feeling that pulsed in her chest.

"Yeah, sorry. I didn't sleep well last night, and I guess I zoned out."

"You sure?" Emma asked with concern.

Izzie forced a smile and nodded, glancing at Alison,

who was studying her soul. It was the first time she had ever felt uncomfortable with it, and she wondered exactly what Alison could tell from it. She needed to sort things out in her head. The vision she saw could have simply been something she had watched on television during summer break or a manifestation of her own fears of the darkness that floated around the school. It had felt very real, though —the exhaustion, the fear, the worry. It had felt like she was right there, doing whatever she was doing, pressed against that red brick wall.

Izzie knew there was something different about her. She knew that her memories weren't the whole story, and more and more often she witnessed different images in her head that made no sense, but for some reason felt like real events. Her magic wasn't like anyone else's, either. It grew stronger every day and had already surpassed some of the more powerful Light Elves she had met. She knew there was a story in there somewhere, that she was more than just a Light Elf, but she had no idea what she could be. Somewhere deep in the back of her mind, she worried that everyone was right. That she was the toombie, and the dark magic was starting to take her over.

Alison watched Izzie's soul flashing all different types of colors. At first, it was contemplative, then suddenly it lit up wildly with many shades of red and yellow. Izzie sat across from her silently, but her soul read like she was in a vicious battle for her life. When Emma had startled her, it had settled down, but the hues of worry still swirled through her. Whatever was going on with her wasn't good, and she hoped she would talk to her about it later.

"So, I was rolling down the street on my skateboard, and the wheel just started wobbling back and forth. I pulled out my wand to fix it, but then I noticed that the neighbors were having a cookout in the front yard. I mean, who has a cookout in the front yard?" Ethan was telling a story from his summer vacation at his aunt's.

"Right?" Luke replied laughing. "What did you do?"

"What else could I do? I shoved the wand back into my pocket and tried to balance. The wheel flew into the other yard, and I flew into the neighbors' metal trashcan. Everyone at the party stopped and stared at me, standing there with trash hanging off my clothes and a lame limp."

The group laughed loudly. They were sitting at a local restaurant having dinner. Ethan shook his head and popped a French fry into his mouth.

"It was horrifying, and to make matters worse, their granddaughter, who is not only my age but hot, was standing there watching the whole thing. We'd actually made plans for that night, but after my tumble through their garbage, she called and canceled. She didn't even make up an excuse."

"Oh, man." Tanner laughed. "That's harsh."

"Tell me about it." Ethan sighed. "Let's just say I don't think I'll end up like Tony Hawk anytime soon."

"More like Ethan Hawke when he did that terrible movie about being a cop, and everybody wanted to wipe their own memory after seeing it." Emma chuckled.

"Or A.J. Hawk from the Cincinnati Bengals and his absolutely terrible podcast." Peter chuckled. "What's that thing called?"

Luke and Ethan answered loudly at the same time in low growling voices, "The Hawk Cast."

Everyone laughed. The girls didn't know who A.J. Hawk was, except for Aya, but she didn't want to admit to her slight obsession with human football. Kathleen looked across the table at Izzie and Alison and both smiled politely, but it was obvious they were lost in their own thoughts.

"Hey, you two." Kathleen threw a fry at them. "Come back to Earth. You've been out of it since the coffee shop."

Izzie shook her head and smiled. "I'm here, I promise."

"I'm just picturing the sequence of events that happened to Ethan over...and over...and over in my head, because it will never get old," Alison replied with a smirk.

Neither of the girls was telling the truth, but they didn't want to admit it. When everyone finished eating they paid their bill and headed to the school bus stop, catching a ride to the roller rink on the edge of town. All of them had, of course, been to one before, but none of them knew the glory of the roller skating rink in the nineties. Well, until they stepped into Roller Rink-O-Rama.

When they walked through the front door, they all stared. Everything was covered in soft velvet except the floors, which had wild geometrical shapes all over them in bright colors. To the left was a concession stand with a popcorn maker, a Slushee machine, and one of those hot dog cookers with the rollers. To the left were some large round benches, also covered in worn-out velvet, and the skate exchange.

Alison looked at all the souls gliding along around her and having fun. Tanner took her hand and squeezed it, leaning in.

"You look panicked."

"I don't know if the blind girl should try roller skates for the first time in a busy place like this," she whispered.

"Don't worry, I'll help you. It'll just look like you are a really bad skater at first," he replied, rubbing his fingers over her hand.

"Okay, but if I break my tailbone, you are carrying my inflatable donut around." Alison smirked.

"It's a deal." He laughed.

Izzie stood at the counter next to Alison, exchanging their shoes out for a pair of skates. Out on the floor, they heard several people shouting and at least three thuds when people wiped out hard. Izzie saw Claire and Scarlett skating with a look of boredom on their faces while Wyatt and Henry jostled and ribbed several of the younger kids as they plowed around the rink, doing ridiculous dances to the late 90s early 2000's boy bands pumping through the speakers.

Tanner knelt in front of Alison and helped her lace her skates, then pulled her to her feet. She wobbled and he grabbed her arms, chuckling. The lights dimmed, and a DJ came over the speaker.

"Grab the girl you love, wish you could love, or just like for the night, and join us for our first couples skate of the evening."

The lights changed to stars floating back and forth across the floor, and different people paired off and rolled onto the rink. Ethan ended up with Aya and Kathleen on his arm, Peter and Emma awkwardly held hands, Izzie and Luke were speeding around, and Tanner carefully pulled Alison along the outside of the floor, out of the way of the faster skaters.

When the song was about to end, the gang noticed five teenaged wizards and witches roll out on the floor, cutting across to the center. All five of them wore black, and the one who seemed to be the leader had a robe on. The symbol on the back was familiar to Izzie, but she didn't know why. They were dark magical beings, and Alison could see the black magic swirling through them like ink in water.

The wizards and witches pulled out their wands and started firing small balls of dark magic across the floor, hitting several people and sending them tumbling to the ground. Before the chaperones who watched the city during the weekends could stop it, a fight broke out on the floor. Alison pushed her back against the wall and pulled energy in through her arms to the palms of her hands. She sent out sparks of glittering light, hitting one of the wizards and knocking him to the ground. Ethan sped through, going low on one skate and snatching up the wizard's wand.

Izzie was on top of it. Her magic came to her quicker than she could think it through. With one hand she shielded people all over the place from the dark magic flying around, and with the other, she sent a hailstorm of light at them. As she nailed the witch in the chest and knocked her to the ground, a flash of a vision momentarily blinded her. She could hear the shrieks and the low cackles of dark wizards. She looked to her right and her left; she was fighting in some sort of battle. A woman and a man were next to her, but she couldn't see them clearly; only their backs. Lost in the vision, she didn't see the dark magic coming right for her.

"Watch out!" Emma screamed, diving in front of Izzie and trying to shield herself at the same time.

She wasn't able to get the shield up, and the magic struck her hard in the arm. She fell to the ground writhing in pain. Izzie dropped to her knees to help as Professor Hudson ran through with her wand out, casting a massive spell toward the dark wizards and witch. The ball of light swallowed them and slammed them on their backs in the middle of the rink. The boy in the robe stood up angrily and opened a portal that they escaped through before anyone else could attack.

Before she did anything else, she cast a spell on all the humans in the room. *"Never was, Never Will Be."*

Everyone non-magical froze in position. Professor Hudson looked at the magicals and waved her hands.

"Come on. I need everyone's help. This spell will erase the last twenty minutes of their memories, bringing them back to the last thought they had before the dark magic attack. We have to arrange the humans in comfortable positions. Please, nothing profane, and if they are on skates on the floor, make sure they don't run into a wall as soon as they unfreeze."

Everyone ran around the rink, pulling and pushing on the humans, moving their limbs like they were mannequins. Elias Hodges darted out on the floor, knelt next to Izzie, and looked at Emma. She was crying, holding her arm and shaking her head.

"She's got a broken arm," he said, carefully picking her up and cradling her in his arms. "I am going to get her back to the school in my car where they can better treat this."

Izzie nodded. She could not believe that she had frozen so badly that one of her friends had to jump in front of a magic bullet to shield her. She was definitely going to have to get Emma a thank you gift or card or something. She'd never had friends like that in her life before, or at least she couldn't remember it. She hugged Luke as Emma disappeared into Elias's arms.

Once the students were back on the bus, it was incredibly loud. They were excited, talking all at once about what had happened. The bus driver, who was a human, gripped the steering wheel tightly and sneered into the rearview mirror.

After about ten minutes, he put up his hands and yelled,

"I will not move this bus until everyone is quiet! I will sit here for the rest of the night if I have to, but I cannot deal with all the noise. Sit down and be quiet so I can get you back to the school."

Professor Hudson sighed and leaned toward Professor Fowler. "Then we're never going anywhere. We'll all die right here in these seats."

The noise level began to drop almost immediately, but there were still several girls toward the back who whispered and giggled loudly. It was even more obvious since everyone else was silent. Professor Hudson took a deep breath and patiently waited, trying to let the driver come to his own place of Zen and get them back to the school. However, after about ten more minutes and the annoying echoes of student shushing each other, she flicked her wand by her knees, calming the driver down.

He blinked and relaxed his shoulders, then reached forward and started the bus. Everyone cheered but he didn't even notice. He was in his own blissful place. Professor Hudson smiled and sat back, looking at Professor Fowler.

"He seems to have changed his tune," she said, raising an eyebrow and glancing down at the wand in the professor's lap.

She quickly put the wand in the inside pocket of her coat and crossed her arms over her chest.

"You can judge me all you want, but being trapped in a bus with all these magical teenagers sounds like the worst kind of hell I can imagine. I'd rather spell the guy than claw my way out of here, hurting people in the process. It happens once a semester. It's not a magic thing, actually.

It's a 'too many hormones packed into a moving tin can' kind of thing."

"Hey, I don't blame you at all. I was considering a spell that sewed their mouths shut, so it's probably good that you beat me to the punch."

14

After everyone got back to the school, they all went into the cafeteria for ice cream sundaes. Although Alison and Izzie were ready for a quiet walk, they wouldn't skip out on Ice Cream Day. It was everything to them, and they'd waited all summer to make their own sundaes again. The only person who didn't come along was Luke, who excused himself so he could get some sleep before another day of tryouts. He was exhausted from being up all night, the tryouts themselves, and the restraint he'd had to show at the battle in the Roller-O-Rama. The last thing they'd needed was for him to wolf out in a pair of roller skates. It would have been disastrous. Amusing, but disastrous nonetheless.

The rest of the group sat around enjoying their ice cream and replaying Emma's harrowing attempt to save Izzie' s life. She was still in the medical clinic, and the teachers had said they couldn't visit until the next day. She was resting comfortably on whatever pain medication they had given her. As each one finished, they excused themselves for bed until the only three left were Izzie, Alison, and Tanner. Tanner rubbed his stomach. He had a smudge of chocolate on the corner of his mouth. Izzie motioned to him so he would know, and he wiped it quickly away.

"You ladies going to bed?"

"I think Izzie and I are going to grab some girl-time and go out for a walk. It's the Faery Festival tonight. The faeries from Oriceran visit for one or two nights and they have like a ritual dance and flight to wish luck on the plants and animals for wintertime on Earth. They do it on Oriceran too, but they started coming to Earth as well since winters can be so harsh here." Izzie was stoked, but even more so because she got to hang out with her best friend.

"Sounds....interesting." He chuckled. "Then I will leave you two and go to bed."

"Goodnight." Alison smiled as he kissed her cheek.

Izzie and Alison finished their sundaes and headed quietly outside, not wanting anyone to follow them. Headmistress Berens had told Izzie about the faeries, knowing she and Alison would venture out there to enjoy the show. They trekked through the courtyard and over the hills until they reached one that overlooked the orchards below. Alison could already see the glow of magical energy floating through the branches, as well as flashes of energy that she figured were small portals the faeries used to travel from Oriceran to Earth.

The girls sat down on the cool ground and Alison brought her knees to her chin, wrapping her arms around her legs. Izzie leaned her head on Alison's shoulder as the faeries appeared, fluttering through the branches of the fruit trees and swirling through the air in a show of sparkling blue, purple, and green lights. The faeries were prepared for a fun evening exploring the old forests of Charlottesville, and casting magical luck spells on all the foliage to shroud it from the coming frozen winter.

Izzie sat up and crossed her legs in front of her, leaning back on her hands. "I wonder what it's like to be one of those faeries? They are so beautiful."

The faeries were some of the loveliest creatures on Oriceran. They were only about five inches tall, with delicate wings that glowed different colors. They had cherubic faces and wore little green outfits, kind of like Tinker Bell.

"I bet it's a blast, flying through the air, always singing, always happy."

"Mara said that some years the Queen of the Faeries comes to the celebration. Her light shines gold, and brighter than any of the other faeries out there. When she sings the trees and grass bend toward her, drawn to the natural essence she puts out."

"That would be neat to sense." Alison smiled. "Do you think she will come tonight?"

"I think it depends on what kind of winter she thinks we are going to have. She usually only comes when it will be a bad winter."

The girls sat there for a good part of the night, watching the faeries play and listening to them sing as they cast their spells over the grounds. Alison loved it. She watched their energies swirl together, shooting across the air. It was what she imagined shooting stars looked like, only way cooler with the bright colors and careful, graceful movements.

To Izzie it was calming, something that made her feel like there was still some good in the world, even if it had come from another one. She didn't remember ever seeing a faerie before, but she loved the pictures of them in Mara's books. When Mara found out, she made sure to let Izzie know about the castings that year, and Izzie had been waiting patiently for that very night.

The songs of the faeries were comforting too. The music was mild and carefree, and their voices floated through the air like soft flower petals.

Izzie sighed. "I feel like if they put out an album, I would never stop listening to it. It makes me feel like I could never do harm to anyone or anything."

Alison giggled. "That's the song of the faeries. It's supposed to do that. They sing because they love to, but also because it stops their enemies or anyone from hunting them down for a tasty snack. My mom used to tell me stories about them, and how she made friends with some of them as a kid."

"That's so cool." Izzie smiled and shook her head. "I hope I can visit Oriceran one day."

"Tanner goes sometimes," Alison replied. "Or he used to. I can't remember what he told me."

"You really like him, don't you?" Izzie smiled.

"I do, and it kind of came out of nowhere. When I saw him that day in my meditation and again in real life, I knew there was a reason for it. I knew the planet was trying to tell me something. When I sat down with him, it was like instant comfort. There was this draw, and I couldn't beat around the bush. I felt comfortable telling him everything."

"That's how things are with Luke." Izzie sighed. "Like

we can say anything to each other, and it doesn't matter since we won't judge. When I saw him that night as a shifter, I seriously got lost in his eyes. For a moment, we were the only two people there. I thought maybe it had something to do with his wolf, but from what I've read about them, they don't put off any magical attraction. I don't know. It's hard to explain, but it's like we were meant to be there together."

"You don't have to try. I totally get it."

"Anyway." Izzie giggled, catching herself getting a bit too mushy. "Are you glad that we are one grade higher this year?"

"Yes! Not that it's that much different. We still have to deal with the asshole upperclassmen, but at least the classes are more interesting."

"And all the extracurricular stuff like the play. Oh, speaking of that, you never told me what you are going to be doing for the talent show."

"I've actually never told anyone." Alison smirked.

"What do you mean?"

"I kind of have this hidden talent, and the only person who knew was my mother. I haven't even told Shay or Brownstone."

"What is it? Can you like play the wine glasses or juggle while balancing on one hand, all of which would be even more impressive if people knew you were blind." Izzie giggled.

"True." Alison laughed. "But it's none of those. Actually, it's simple. I can sing."

"You can *sing*? Are you serious?"

"Yeah, and I know it's not crazy, because Emma told me

about your heavenly voice that broke hearts all over the auditorium."

"Yeah." Izzie scoffed. "Right before I almost broke bodies with my uncontrollable temper tantrum."

"Meh. If nothing else, it gave you some street cred." Alison laughed.

"So what kind of stuff do you sing?"

"Anything really, but my favorite is like 20s to 40s blues and jazz."

"Whoa, that's impressive."

Alison laughed, pretty sure that was exactly the response she was going to get. She pulled herself to her feet and turned to face Izzie's soul.

"How about I give you a little taste? You can tell me if I should forego my debut on the stage."

"Oooh, yeah, sing for me! What are you going to sing?"

"I'll sing one of my favorites, by a jazz singer name Connee Boswell. It's called *The Object of my Affection*. I think Dean Martin sang it too, but I like the girl version better."

"Of course." Izzie laughed.

"Okay, here goes."

Alison put her hand on her stomach, closed her eyes, and took a deep breath. She wasn't nervous, not around Izzie, but she had never sung in front of anyone except her mother—and that had been a long time before.

"The object of my affection can change my complexion
From white to rosy red..."

Izzie's mouth dropped open as this voice erupted from Alison's body. It was almost like there was another woman inside her singing the lyrics. She was completely and totally surprised and wanted her to continue.

Izzie closed her eyes and swayed back and forth to the song, loving it, especially with the hum in the background. She opened her eyes when she realized it wasn't just the sounds of nature, but the faeries. They had stopped singing when they heard Alison and started to hum along with her singing. Izzie laughed and shook her head as the faeries flew up to where the girls were and started flying in brightly colored circles around them, their wings twinkling and sparkling wildly.

Alison opened her eyes as she sang the chorus, really feeling it deep down in her soul. She smiled, focusing on the energy of the hundreds of faeries who flew around her. They sang with her, giving her a background, and made the moment perfect. When she finished the last note of the song, the faeries fluttered their wings loudly and hovered for just a moment before flying back down to the orchard. Alison sat back down beside Izzie and both the girls let out deep breaths, followed by a chorus of giggles.

"At least you know that there are hundreds of faeries out there who will stop doing their magic just to listen to you sing." Izzie laughed.

"I know, right? That was absolutely insane."

"Well, I think you know the answer. You are going to rock it out there on that stage."

15

Time was rolling by, and the season quickly changed to fall. Everyone was enamored with the colors shimmering in trees across the grounds. The leaves fluttered in wild colors: oranges, yellows, and browns. It was absolutely gorgeous outside, with bright blue skies and the perfect cool, crisp breeze blowing across the courtyard.

Everyone enjoyed walking outside with a warm coffee in hand before heading in for breakfast. The sounds of boots and shoes crunching through the leaves echoed all around them, and the crew was determined to enjoy it while it lasted. In Virginia fall lingered, gradually bringing the icy days of winter up the Blue Ridge Mountains of Albemarle County. Alison and Izzie opted for hot chocolate, and they sat on one of the benches staring at the people.

Ethan was busy helping Horace trim the hedges for one of the last times before winter, and it was obvious that he had no idea what he was really doing. It wasn't volunteer work, that was for sure. It was punishment for pulling a magical prank on one of the freshmen. He'd been practicing for April Fool's, which was still months and months away. He thought every prickly stick that jabbed him in the hand was worth it after seeing the look on the freshman's face when the pictures in his textbook popped out and ran down the hallway. Remnants of the spell—mostly little paper-like creatures that lurked in the corners and grabbed unsuspecting students' ankles— could still be found all around the school.

Mara and the other professors had worked tirelessly to round them all up, but the student refused to come out of his dorm room for two days afterward, too afraid the paper dragon would breathe paper fire at him again. It might have been paper fire, but it had set the collar of his robe aflame.

"Seriously, I am pretty sure that things are going to go well for me this season," Luke said as he walked across the grounds with Peter.

They both looked at Ethan as they passed and gave him a thumbs-up. He lifted his shears in the air triumphantly, only to have Horace grab his arm and pull it back down to the bushes. The guys laughed and continued walking.

"You really seem to love this sport. I mean, I think it's cool. It's like a virtual D&D or something. I just don't have the athletic prowess to play the game."

"Yeah, it's kind of like that in a way. I don't know. I just love how it tests your mind and your body at the same time. The tryouts are so long, though. I feel like they are endless. I just want to get to the field behind the mansion and into a real game, even if it's just against my teammates.

The whole getting-used-to-the-feel-of-the-game thing is getting old. I'm used to it already."

Before lunch, the group had spells class with Eleanor Hudson. It was the second-year version, and they were super-excited about it. The first year was basics, but this year they had actually started diving into some harder spells. They started today's class with a spell to get their juices flowing. They were to move different objects from one podium to another.

Aya was a champion at this and didn't even have to pull magic in to do it. She had been doing it with her dolls her entire life. The rest of the class had varying degrees of success, but unlike most classes, no one made a complete mess or dropped anything. Even Ethan was successful. This time he actually focused on what he was doing instead of sitting back and ignoring the details. After the disaster the year before when he couldn't get the statue cloaked he'd started paying attention, at least in those two classes. In others like history he fell asleep most days, and the rest he spent whittling pieces of wood under his desk.

About halfway through the class, Professor Hudson raised her hand in the air to get everyone's attention.

"Okay, class, since you are doing so well at this, let's move on to a harder spell. This one will help you read magical trails, which can tell you where the being is going. It's a form of tracking that is used almost daily by bounty hunters. For the spell, everyone, no matter how you muster your magic, you focus on the trails, release a thin fog, and say the casting either out loud or in your head. The words are '*Trackius Beings.*'"

Everyone started attempting the spell, and Alison stood next to Izzie, watching her soul and the energy flowing from her magic as she easily picked it up. Izzie saw the trails of many different magical beings, but because it was the school, there were almost too many to focus on. They shimmered and moved, different colors signifying different magical beings. She slowly turned in a circle, fascinated by them all. As she went past the door she stopped, noticing a dark magic trail in the hall, spotty and a bit older, but definitely from the current school year. She followed it out of the room and crouched, running her finger across it.

"What do you see?" Eleanor asked, following her into the hall.

"It's a dark trail," Izzie replied.

Eleanor looked at Izzie with concern for a moment, then did her own casting, lighting up the trail for everyone to see. She was curious about it, and wondered if it had any connection to the things that had occurred in the town. As the dark trail shimmered into view, Mara walked out of one of the classrooms and did a double-take. She slowly walked forward and looked at Izzie, realizing she had been the one to find it.

"What intruder has been on the grounds?" she whispered to herself. "And what does Izzie remember that opened this up for her?"

Eleanor looked up and saw Mara standing there, her eyes narrowed, staring at Izzie with interest and concern. It wasn't a look of fear or suspicion, but one of caring and question. It wasn't the time to approach Mara about it, but she made a mental note to look into it later. Something was going on, between the dark trail and Mara's reaction, and though she knew it probably wasn't her business, she was a professor at the school and wanted to know what they might be facing.

"Izzie," Eleanor began, standing up. "What did you see leading up to the dark trail?"

Izzie stood up before answering. "Um, there were several light magic trails, and then it went blank for a few moments, and then the dark trail went through, and then a pause, and then more light trails."

"Okay, and did it give you a feeling?"

Izzie shook her head. "No, not like dark magic usually does."

"That could mean that the trail is older, not from the last week or so."

She questioned Izzie while trying not to draw attention to them as the other students practiced inside, but she needed answers to try to figure out who the intruder was. They hadn't been inside the classroom, so the culprit wasn't in there and it certainly wasn't Izzie. If she *were* a toombie, she would know she had the darkness and could have very well been looking at her own trail. That settled Eleanor's nerves a bit.

Izzie bent down and touched the trail again, closing her eyes. "Whoever this is, they came and they went, but they didn't linger too long here. They aren't in the school any longer."

"That's what I was feeling; like it was a short visit, for whatever reason."

"Yes, but I can't tell who exactly the intruder was."

"That's way more difficult to do, and takes a lot of practice."

Eleanor marveled to herself at Izzie's abilities and her conclusions that the intruder had come and gone. Eleanor could tell, but for someone of Izzie's age with minimal experience doing magic, the fact that she could see it at all and read it so accurately was shocking. She hadn't met a magical being like that since she had met Mara's granddaughter Leira when she came to speak at the school. Her powers had gradually come into play, then *bam*—they had erupted quickly after that. It seemed to be happening to Izzie, too.

"Why don't we follow this trail?"

"All right." Izzie nodded.

Eleanor and Izzie walked through the school, slowly following the dark magic trail, Mara watching them walk away. The trail went down the hall, circled through the cafeteria, and went up the steps and through the dorms. It looped around several times, but never stopped in one place for too long. Eleanor knew they had been there and where they had gone, but had absolutely no idea why they had come. When they got back to the classroom, the other students were still trying the spell, too excited about the new ability to notice anything else.

Alison, however, had noticed and overheard them. When they had walked off to follow the trail she stood in the hall, pulled her magic up, and attempted to see the soul and energy of whoever had left the trail. Most dark magical beings cleaned up their tracks, but this person hadn't, which meant that either they wanted the trail to be seen, or they didn't know how to cover it. It could also be the case that they had no idea they were dark and had left the trail without knowing. Since they weren't still there, the last one was a bit of a stretch. It took a long time and a lot of change to move the dark energy out of you, and you really had to want to be light, something that obviously didn't happen very often.

Alison tried to see the figure, but couldn't. She could only see the souls that were still present, and whoever this person was, they were long gone. Izzie came back and stood next to Alison, her arms crossed in front of her.

"I tried to see their soul," Alison whispered. "But I can only see people who are still here. It's obvious that this person is not."

"Yeah, I could see their trail, but it ends," Izzie replied. "I don't feel the dark magic in here either. They would have to have a lot of it in them to leave a trail that distinct and have it last like that."

"Whoever it was, they were looking for something," Alison said with a sigh.

"Or someone." Izzie shivered just thinking about it. "You know what?"

"What?" Alison asked.

"With your ability to see souls and energy and my ability to track dark magic, we make one hell of a strong team."

"I know, right? We could become detectives and be partners. We could solve crimes faster than anyone else."

"We would be the new Leira Berens." Izzie giggled.

They stood there for a couple more minutes before Izzie put her arm through Alison's and squeezed her hand.

"We should get back inside before someone notices us hanging out in the hall. I'm sure that if I can see the dark trail, someone else can too."

"Don't underestimate yourself. There are not a lot of strong and talented people like you. You have something they don't."

"Yeah," Izzie replied walking into the classroom. "It just would be nice to know what it is."

16

Finding the gumption to keep up their spirits with Emma still in the hospital was starting to be a challenge for the group. They hadn't realized how much it would affect them when one of their teammates went down, and Izzie had already visited several times and covered her corner in the sick bay with all kinds of magical flowers. Emma told her to stop worrying so much, that she would have done the same for her, but Izzie still felt bad when she was laid up with a broken arm and concussion while Izzie was going to class.

"Hey, it's like a vacation," Emma told her. "They even let me watch television, like the old-school human game shows. They are *hilarious*. Did you know people used to dress up in wacky costumes and try to get things from their bags so that the host would pick them to play a game where most of the time they lost anyway?"

"Sounds weird." Izzie giggled, rolling her eyes as the bell rang after lunch.

"Go to class. I can't believe you missed lunch just for me."

Izzie winked. "I won't starve. Get out of jail soon. We miss you."

"I miss you guys, too."

Izzie made her way out of the sick bay and down the hallway toward her class. Luke came out of the cafeteria and tossed Izzie a baggie with a half a sandwich and a cut up apple in it. She smiled and waited for him to catch up.

"How did you manage that?"

"I explained it to my plate. Yes, I just said I talked to my plate. Hey, it worked."

"Mmm, egg salad, my favorite."

"The mighty plate knows all."

Izzie giggled as they made their way to their next class. They walked inside and took the last empty seats, one in front of the other. Elias Hodges, looking as suave as ever, stood at the front of the class and smiled.

"I know, I know, Transfiguration Class is everyone's favorite," he joked.

A few people laughed, and one let out a loud whoop. Elias pointed at the kid in the back with a smile, and the girls giggled. Alison wondered just how handsome this guy actually was. His soul was definitely shrouded with suavity, but so was Max Regency's—and he was not bringing in the girls.

"All right, so to me transfiguration is a complete change of form or appearance into a more beautiful or spiritual state," Elias explained. "Like shifters."

Several people in the class snickered and scoffed. Elias stood up straight, putting his hands in his pockets, and frowned. He hated how much shifters were disliked. It wasn't because of what they did, but because of the stigma that continued to be passed from generation to generation. If parents stopped hating, he would eventually have a class that understood what he was trying to tell them. He was tired of watching the shifters in his class hang their heads in shame.

Elias scanned the room, flashing yellow through his eyes that quieted everyone on the spot. They might snicker and scoff, but some were terrified of the wolves. Izzie seemed curious to Elias, but then again, she could always be found at Luke's side. Elias's eyes shifted to Luke, who looked down at his lap and twiddled his thumbs. Elias took a deep breath and sat on the edge of his desk.

"There is a beauty to the shape and form of a wolf as it transforms from an everyday state to an animal that is sleek and strong and has eyes sharper than any other creature and hearing that could track a footstep a hundred miles away if it wanted to. Trolls are the same way, for that matter. They start out as these little furry things with sharp teeth and can grow taller or shorter, morph into the shape of a dog or cat or even a very large toucan. While the shifter changes completely, no matter what the troll turns into, he keeps the same fur and teeth. I think of the troll as the Cheshire cat of Oriceran; always watching and quiet, but incredibly intelligent and sneaky."

"And a pain in the ass," one of the guys yelled.

"Yes." Elias chuckled, happy to be off the subject of shifters. "If you do anything to save a troll from harm, they bond with you for life. The magic bond even goes so far that if the master dies, the troll dies too. They can feed off their person's emotions, sometimes uncontrollably, but they are faithful, funny, smart, and very, very wise. In the wild, a troll can live close to a thousand years if they aren't eaten by a larger predator."

"If they can shift into anything, how does any creature best them?"

"Everyone has weaknesses and vulnerabilities. Take the wolves. Even without the use of everyday magic like a wizard or elf; they can beat you in a battle because they have the numbers and the strength. However, if it is one on one or a shifter is caught right as it changes, it can't react faster than magic. Similarly, most magical beings—except perhaps a Kilomea—cannot react with enough strength once a wolf pounces on them."

"But they attack for no reason."

"That's the rumor, but have you ever actually read a story where one attacked for no reason? Have you seen it?"

Izzie put up her hand. "I had a shifter in wolf form walk right in front of me, and it let me run my hand through its fur."

Ethan yelled, "I hear Leira Berens has a whistle, and if she uses it the shifters come to the rescue immediately."

"They are mangy mutts," one of the assholes blurted. "And an accident on Oriceran."

Everyone looked at the kid and Izzie was tempted pull some power, but when she looked at Elias, he shook his head.

"Well, in this class you are going to learn all about shifters and other creatures that transfigure, and hopefully, we can change your mind by the end."

"Yeah, right." Luke scoffed under his breath. "We'll live and die as outcasts."

That broke Izzie's heart.

The library was packed full of sophomores spending their free period in study hall. They weren't even sure why it was called a free period since they were required to be in study hall and were given detention if found anywhere else. It was the day before the start of their fall break, and though they were expected to be quiet and reading, none of them could focus well enough. They all wanted to talk about what they planned to do during their vacations. Even Alison was excited to go home this time.

"Izzie, what are you going to do? You should come home with me. Brownstone and Shay wouldn't mind." Alison sighed.

"No, no, I have plenty to do. I think I might go and investigate the kemana more. It's not like the last time I was there we really got to see a lot."

"True. We were kind of...invisible." Alison giggled.

"Yeah, but we saved an unappreciative little punk from getting eaten by a Kilomea, or whatever they do to their victims."

"I don't think they eat them. That would be slightly cannibalistic, but I'm sure that the person probably wishes they were getting eaten by the end of it."

"I still can't believe he was so ungrateful."

"I know, right?" Izzie laughed. "I felt like throwing him back down the staircase to fend for himself."

Emma looked up and smiled, leaning forward on her books. "Alison, what are you and your wards going to do?"

Alison smiled proudly, actually having something to tell people for once. "Well, my dad and my Aunt Shay..."

"Wait, wait, wait." Aya stopped her. "Your *dad?*"

"Yeah." Alison giggled. "I might have forgotten to mention it, but over summer break Brownstone adopted me."

Aya covered her mouth to stifle a squeal. "That is so amazing."

"Sorry I didn't mention it. There was so much going on when we got back. Yeah, so anyway, my *DAD* and Aunt Shay are taking me to this resort kemana for the whole time. I hear it's like one of the best times you can have beneath the Earth."

"I've heard about that place," Kathleen whispered. "They supposedly enchant the ceiling of the caves to look like the blue sky of the tropics during the day and the Oriceran sky at night."

The librarian walked over and swatted the desk with a rolled-up piece of paper, he and his flower making shushing faces. The girls grimaced and went back to pretending to study. Alison sighed and clutched her back-pack. She was nervous and scared to bring it into the open and talk about it. What if they scoffed at her or made fun of her? She had a hard time imagining that from her friends, but she had lived through much crazier things that she hadn't seen coming.

She looked at the souls of her friends, knowing she had to tell them before she left for break. They were at a secluded table in the front section where no one else would overhear, and they were all together. There wouldn't be a better time than right then to get it done. She took a deep breath and leaned forward, shaking her hands to get their attention. She could see streams of curiosity flow through each soul as the group stared at her, letting her know she had the room, or at least the table.

She swallowed hard and shook her head, speaking in a hushed tone. "Guys, there is something that I want to talk to you about. I've wanted to tell you all semester, but I guess I've just been kind of scared about it. I didn't know how you would react."

"You can tell us anything." Emma smiled.

"Yeah, A, spill it. We're all ears," Ethan replied in a kind tone.

"Well, you all know by now that I am a Drow."

They all muttered yes, waiting for her to go on.

"That gives me a special sight that really comes in handy. One other fun fact..." She wrung her hands nervously. "Here goes. I'm blind. I can see energy, souls, and magic, but that's it."

Everyone looked at each other sheepishly, not saying a word. She sat there trying to figure out what their reactions were, but couldn't hear anything or see anything in their souls. She was starting to get really nervous.

"Guys, don't just sit there. She told you she can't see you. Say something." Izzie glared at them, tilting her head.

"What is it?" Alison asked nervously. "Just say it. Whatever you want to say, I can take it."

Kathleen sighed. "Aya already blabbed."

Aya turned bright red and reached out taking Alison's hand. "I'm so sorry. I just thought it would be easier if everyone knew. That way if you needed any help with anything, they would know. And with all the fights and dark magic, having a blind partner is kind of important to understand. They were completely blown away, though, when I told them."

Alison started, then broke out into laughter, covering her mouth so she wouldn't be too loud.

Ethan reached out and squeezed Alison's hand. "We wanted to give you a chance tell us when you were ready."

"You guys are great." Alison chuckled. "You are like my second family."

Kathleen raised an eyebrow. "Like?"

Izzie pouted. "Second?"

Alison giggled and put her arms around Izzie and squeezed, whispering into her ear. "You are my sister through and through; don't ever think anything different." Then, "You *are* my family. All of you are."

She let go of Izzie and put her hand out, the rest of them squeezing it. "Thank you, guys. You are the best."

17

The group met in the lobby, everyone with bags packed and ready to leave for their fall break. Everyone but Izzie, but she was going to accompany them to the train station to see them off. She and Mara would be staying behind at the school, since the headmistress had business to attend to. Izzie would be left to her own devices, and planned to check in on Marigold and help Horace around the grounds. Though she didn't mind, she was going to miss her friends, but at least the school now felt like home to her.

When Peter finally made it down, having packed more than he probably needed, the group went out to the front gate and caught the jitney to Charlottesville. On the bus ride over Izzie listened to Kathleen complain because she had to go back to her actual house—more like a mansion— instead of going on an extravagant trip. Emma was just happy to be seeing her parents for a few days, Aya was the same, and Ethan was headed to Peter's house. Izzie

JUDITH BERENS

wondered if the two of them were going to drive Peter's family mad or literally blow them right off the foundation.

"We are working on a project for the club," Peter explained. "It has the possibility of helping so many people if we can get it right."

"Not to mention, it would make us enough money that we wouldn't ever have to work again."

"And what would you do with your time?" Kathleen asked. "Video games?"

"I would be one of those adventure seekers, skydiving, jumping off buildings, or whatever I could find."

"I dunno, doesn't seem too adventurous with your wand in your hand for safety." Emma giggled.

"I'll leave my wand at home."

"You are part elf," Kathleen scoffed. "You can't leave that at home."

The bus pulled up in Charlottesville and let the students off at the Starbucks. They passed a normal couple, who shook their heads and stared at the gaggle of people inside the Starbucks.

"I swear, no matter where we go the Starbucks are constantly packed, and half the people I see don't have drinks. I don't get it. Is it like the cool place to hang out?"

Ethan smirked as they walked by, holding the door for the others. Izzie followed them down to the platform and saw each person off, since all of them were headed in different directions. Alison stood in front of her, watching the thin blue streaks swirl through her soul.

"You sure you don't want to come with me? It will be fun. You can learn martial arts from Brownstone."

She smiled. "I'll be fine. I'm really looking forward to

exploring the grounds and spending some time with the horses."

"Okay," Alison replied, leaning in and kissing her cheek. "Don't get in any trouble while I'm gone."

Izzie laughed. "I'll try not to."

She waved, her hair blowing wildly as Alison's train whooshed down the tracks into the darkness. She sighed and patted her hands on her legs, turned around, and climbed the stairs back to the top. She grabbed a coffee from the Starbucks and decided to go over to the mall and mill about, despite Mara's directive not to do things alone in town because it wasn't safe. It was just the mall, which was full of people so Izzie couldn't see what the harm could be.

She took the jitney to the mall and walked around, reading the magical histories and wandering through some of the shops. She grabbed fun foods like giant pretzels and kabobs, things she could munch on while she strolled. She left one of the candle stores smelling like cotton, freshly washed clothes, and a leather men's candle. As she turned the corner, she froze at the sight of the dark wizards from earlier in the year.

Again, without warning her stomach turned, and she felt herself drifting at the edge of a memory. She put her hands on her head, feeling pressure, and closed her eyes. There she was again, near two people she could only see from behind, fighting someone in the distance. That vision faded and the other started—her leaning against a brick wall, sweaty and tired, dark magic flying by and someone screaming in the background.

She took a deep breath and pushed the visions back,

stumbling to a bench. There wasn't enough of a memory to understand what was happening, but whatever it was it was serious. She rubbed her forehead and made herself calm down, pulling a bottle of water from her bag and taking small, slow sips.

These visions were getting worse each time, and even more frustrating since she couldn't put the pieces together. Who were those people? They vaguely looked like the ones she had remembered the year before, what she could see of them, during her memory of a holiday dinner at that couple's house when she was younger. It was hard to be sure, though. All she could see were their backs. In the vision, as soon as they started to turn it cut out.

Izzie wondered if she should tell Mara. After all, she was her legal guardian. Then again, it would worry her, and put an even bigger strain on Izzie's freedom. She figured it was better to just wait for Alison to come back and tell her, or even possibly Horace. Even if they didn't have answers, they would be comforting. She wasn't really sure how much more of it she could take.

Alison met Shay and Brownstone when she got off the train in LA. They'd arranged to catch a plane to Miami and go from there to the kemana resort. She wished they could travel by magical train. It would have been so much faster; ten minutes and they would be basking in the Florida sunlight, but it was impossible, so after they'd hugged hello, they headed back up through the Starbucks.

Brownstone had rented a driver to take them to the

airport in LA. Alison had originally just told them she would meet them in Miami, but Brownstone was too nervous that he wouldn't get there in time, or someone would follow her. He was a bit paranoid at times, but it made sense after everything they had been through. She was just excited about her first family vacation with them.

During the whole plane ride to Miami, Brownstone slept reclined with his inflatable neck pillow around his big neck. Shay sat next to the window, and Alison was in the middle with her head on Brownstone's shoulder. She went into a meditative state, wanting to make sure she was as rested as possible before her vacation. She didn't want to miss a thing.

When she came out of her meditative state, the plane was starting its descent into the Miami airport. Alison poked Brownstone, and he opened his eyes, looking around wildly.

"Huh? What? Is it time for pretzels?"

"No, Dad." Alison giggled.

"You snored your way through the in-flight snack." Shay chuckled. "We are landing in Miami!"

"Yes," he said, pulling the tab on his pillow, the air he squeezed out hitting Alison in the face.

They landed and exited the plane, then grabbed their luggage and found the car they had rented. Brownstone pulled out a hand-drawn map and stared down at it, shrugging.

"We got this, right?"

Shay rolled her eyes and climbed into the passenger seat. To everyone's surprise, though, they made their way straight to the kemana. The entrance sat right outside the city near the back of a public park. They walked along with their bags, and Alison sensed the energy from the kemana below her. There was a blue hue to the ground, and as they approached a long row of trees, the energy swirled up and around, pooling in the center of a knot in a nearby tree.

"How do we get into this thing?" Brownstone grumbled, shifting through the papers in his pockets for the instructions.

Alison wandered over to the tree and pressed her finger into the glowing blue orb in the knot. She hit something hard—a button—and pressed it. Suddenly the ground trembled, and she rushed back over to Shay's and Brownstone's sides. The trees shook wildly and the lush green moss on the forest floor slowly opened, revealing stairs that led into a dark pit. Blue sconces lit the walls, and a cool ocean breeze blew their hair around them. To Alison's sight, it was a sparkling blue hole leading into the magic of the kemana.

They picked up their bags and started down the stairs. Alison felt the charge of energy coming from the stone that was the center of the kemana. When they reached the bottom, a goblin wearing a bright Hawaiian shirt and his bowler hat stood on a stool at a podium.

He nodded. "Mr. Brownstone. Please come on in. The resort check-in is to your right, and the city is straight ahead. If you have any questions, please don't hesitate to ask."

Alison had wandered forward and was gazing at all the energy swirling around the place. Everything had some sort of magic, and the colors she saw created an almost perfect painting of her surroundings. Shay caught up with her, whispering a description of the place.

"There's a magic ocean, a beach, and ziplines across the very, *very* high ceilings of the cave. The sky looks bright blue and has barely any clouds, and wild Oriceran flowers are planted throughout."

"Wow."

"From what I hear there's a pool, water skiing, snorkeling in the magical ocean, shops, and exotic food," Brownstone added, rubbing his belly and walking ahead to hold the doors to the resort open. "First, though, let's get settled in the rooms."

After they put their things away, Alison joined them on the balcony. She looked at the shimmering blue energy that made up the magical ocean in front of them. She wondered for a moment if it was as beautiful to regular eyes as it was to hers.

She sat down in the lounge chair between Shay and Brownstone and let out a deep breath of relaxation.

"How is school going?" Brownstone asked.

"Good. I've got A's in all my classes."

"Excellent. And how about boys? Are you seeing anyone?"

Alison shook her head and kept her lips closed, wisely not saying a word about Tanner. "Did you know that we have a winter formal this year?"

"Oh, really?" Shay said loudly, helping her change the subject.

"Yeah, but I figure I'll probably be too busy studying to go."

Brownstone seemed happy with that answer. Shay held

back a laugh and squeezed her hand. "Aw, that's too bad. Why don't we send you home with a dress anyway? You know, just in case there is no homework, and you are still way ahead."

"Okay." Alison smirked.

She was glad when Shay was around for those awkward moments.

18

Brownstone, Shay, and Alison perused the shops along the strip. Brownstone looked at a bright blue shirt with flamingos and beach chairs on it and held it up in front of himself in the mirror. Shay shook her head, laughing as she patted him on the shoulder. Alison couldn't see what he held up, but she could only imagine. Shay leaned in and whispered, "Think the brightest blue you can imagine, with feathered birds and beach chairs."

"Oh, God." Alison grimaced, then giggled.

She ran her hand over a ribbed sundress, wondering what color it was. She liked the feel of the fabric, and the way the neck was cut in and high with little straps. She ran her hand to the bottom and put it back, knowing there was no way her dad would let her buy a dress that short.

Shay walked past the front of the store, and near the open door felt the cool breeze blowing in. She stopped and stared at three men sticking out like sore thumbs on the street. They were dressed all in black, the material of their robes showing a strange crest on the backs of the high necks. They were carrying their wands openly.

"Brownstone," she whispered. "Come here."

Brownstone hung up the shirt and walked over, looking at the guys. "Thugs."

"That's what I was thinking."

He narrowed his eyes and stared at the crest on the back of their collars, thinking back to something one of his informants had told him. They weren't just thugs. They were *hired* thugs, magical contractors for a private company. They worked under men who wanted to suppress magic.

Alison walked up behind them and stared at the men's energy. It was very dark and she got chills up her spine, remembering the same kind of energy on the Harriken the year before. Brownstone stepped out under the awning and looked at Shay.

"I heard about these guys. They are scouts on paid assignment, to see how humans might be able to take over the kemana one at a time. Whoever they are working for must have ties to the resort business. Big money for a place like this."

"Should we tell someone?" Alison asked. "Like a kemana official or something?"

"I want to see what they are up to first," Brownstone replied slowly as a local official approached them.

Shay watched as the guy on the end slowly pulled his hand behind him, trying to hide the wand. The official was suspicious and started asking them questions to find out what they were doing down there. The guys played nice at first, trying to trick their way out of it, but they hadn't been too smart, coming in there dressed like the characters from *the Matrix*.

Suddenly the guy in the middle pulled his wand and pointed it at the official. People on all sides of them screamed and scattered. Immediately Shay and Brownstone sprinted forward and stopped between the wizards and the official. The wizards didn't seem at all surprised to see Brownstone, which concerned Shay, but there were too many people around to allow a fight like that to break out.

The wizard poked his wand into Brownstone's chest.

"This is none of your business, human," he growled.

The wizard to the left looked nervous, putting his hands up. "We don't want any trouble, Brownstone. We're on official business that doesn't concern you."

"The hell it doesn't," Brownstone barked. "You are trying to take the kemana from the magicals, and well, I just can't let that happen."

Alison listened closely, getting angrier the longer the wizard left his wand poked into her dad's chest. She could see the dark energy swirling around it as it pushed at Brownstone's soul. She started to walk forward, her energy surging through her body like never before. The energy in the wand grew stronger, and there was no way she would allow her dad to be harmed.

Brownstone looked at her and put his hand up. "No, Alison!"

At that moment, the wizard twisted the wand back to strike Brownstone. Alison screamed and sprinted forward, lifting her hands. A dark orb shot from her palms and blew through the air like a cloud, encircling the wizard in darkness. While he was blinded, Brownstone used the opening to slug him across the face, knocking the wand out of his hand and into the sandy beginning of the beach.

Alison didn't pause, just let her magic do its thing. A long stream of white light shot out and formed into a silhouette next to one of the other wizards. He looked at it, furrowing his brow, and fired a steady stream of dark magic at Alison. She jumped and levitated while at the same time sending a large ball of fire directly at him. He was unable to dodge, and the ball of sparkling purple fire slammed into his chest.

Shay ran toward him and booted him in the stomach, knocking him the rest of the way to the ground. She kicked the wand from his hand, but he grabbed her leg and flung her over him into the sand. She jumped up and charged him as Alison slowly came back down. A crowd had gathered to watch as Shay fought the agent in hand-to-hand combat, using her martial arts skills to thrash him up and down the sandy sidewalk. He fell and turned over on his belly to scoot forward and grab his wand.

Alison saw the energy surge through the wood as Shay's soul pounced toward him. Alison could tell she wasn't going to be quick enough. She swung her arms from side to side, following the natural rhythm of her magic. Dancing lights flew from her fingertips to swirl around the guy, momentarily distracting him. Before he was able to look back, Shay punched him hard in the face and grabbed the wand as he hit the ground unconscious. She looked over, amazed at Alison, and called to her.

"Good girl. Nice work."

Just then there was a loud thud, Alison turned in time to see her dad's soul smash into the wooden walkway. The wizard lifted his wand, but Alison wasn't going to let anything else happen. She felt the energy buildup in her head and leaned it back, closed her eyes, and rolled her neck. She stiffened, and when she opened her eyes, the souls and energy were brighter than ever. On the outside, her eyes had completely glazed over in a dark grey color as she stared at the wizard standing over Brownstone.

"Put your wand down," she whispered, using a Drow's magic of suggestion without even realizing it.

The wizard looked strangely at Brownstone and lowered his wand to his side. Brownstone frowned and glanced at Alison, seeing the trance she was in.

"Now break it in half," she whispered.

He snapped it in half, sending a jolt of energy straight into his face that knocked him down.

"Alison," Brownstone called, impressed by her magic but slightly frightened by it at the same time. He had never seen anything like it before.

The sound of her dad's voice brought her out of her trance, and she stared at the three unconscious souls on the ground. Brownstone and Shay glanced at each other and together with the local officer, carried the men toward the entrance of the kemana. They tossed the three men into the park and waited as the officer put a spell on them, blocking them from ever entering another kemana again.

When they returned to the resort, they found Alison on a boardwalk bench, staring out at the shimmering blue energy of the magical ocean.

When they reached the bench, Brownstone put his arm around Alison and pulled her close. She laid her head on his chest, feeling the beating of his heart. She wasn't upset.

She was shocked at her own abilities. Without someone there to guide her the powers had built on their own, and when she let go of that control they took over, doing exactly what needed to be done at the time.

"Where did you learn *that* magic?" Brownstone asked.

"I didn't," Alison whispered. "I tried to find information on Drow, but there isn't much in the library at school. I didn't know what to do, so I just let the magic take over."

Brownstone glanced at Shay, who ran her hand down Alison's hair. She couldn't help but notice that during that one fight almost half her hair, from the bottom up, had turned white with silver tips. Her powers were growing faster than she could understand them, but there was no one they could call to help her.

"You are growing in mind, soul, body, and magic," Brownstone told her comfortingly. "It's not something for you to fear, but instead something you should embrace. You know you have these abilities now, so you should be able to recall them even when you are holding on to your own restraint. You're not only a Drow, but you also have royal blood. Be careful of letting the power guide you too much, or you might get lost in it."

Alison nodded her head, completely understanding what he was saying. This fight was one thing. She'd had to do something to save her family, but until she'd let go, she hadn't even been aware of how capable she was. If she hadn't let go, though, someone might have been hurt or even killed. Now she knew some of her capabilities. She knew she needed to learn how to control them, and use them the way she wanted to.

She sat up and took a deep breath, still staring at the energy of the ocean. "Do you know what I want?"

Shay smiled gently. "What's that, sweetie? World peace?"

"Well, yes, but I was thinking of something even greater than that."

"What can be greater than world peace?" Brownstone asked, confused.

Alison turned toward his voice, staring at his large soul. "Ice cream. You know, the kind they make into little ice balls and you can mix all the flavors together?"

Brownstone threw his head back and laughed loudly, squeezing her tightly. "You are a good kid, Alison. I'm proud of you."

Those were probably the best words she had heard in a long time.

19

Suffice it to say, Alison was glad to be back at school. Her vacation had turned out to be a bit more educational than she had hoped. She just wanted her normal routine, and she sank back into the daily life of school pretty fast. Before she knew it, it was Halloween, and the campus was decorated from top to bottom with magical décor. All around the courtyard, magical ghosts swayed in the now-almost-leafless trees. Scattered throughout were tall oil lamps that when lit in the evenings made everything look eerie.

At one of the outside picnic tables, the group talked about what their Halloween costumes would be. The whole school loved that time of year, because instead of being limited to the cheap plastic costumes at the store and bad makeup applications, they could use their magic to turn them temporarily into whatever they wanted to be—without the side effects that becoming a zombie, warlock, or vampire would entail, of course.

"I am going as Queen Victoria," Emma said happily. "I saw a painting of her in one of the history books at my mom's house, and we look really alike. No one has ever been able to prove it, but the rumors were that Prince Albert was a wizard, and that was how he kept Queen Victoria in love with him for so long."

"Maybe you really are her descendant, then," Aya said excitedly.

"Probably not, but I get to wear a really gorgeous dress and a bonnet, so I'm down."

Kathleen smiled. "I'm going as a Sphinx. My dad taught me the magic to make it perfect and lifelike. You won't even be able to tell it's me."

"That's awesome." Izzie smiled. "I really don't know what I want to be yet. How about you, Alison?"

Alison looked up from the table, her mind having drifted back to what had happened at the kemana and the spells that she had cast. "Oh, I'm not sure yet. I was thinking maybe a full-out Drow queen or something."

"But you're already a Drow," Kathleen replied. "Get crazy with it. You should be a sexy vampire goddess or something. You know, something that would make Tanner's jaw drop."

"What about my jaw?" Tanner asked, walking up and sitting next to Alison before giving her a kiss on the cheek.

"Nothing." Alison blushed. "What are you going to be for Halloween?"

"Please don't say a wolf." Ethan chuckled.

He laughed. "No. Izzie promised she would make me into something cool using her magic. I told her she could pick. I trust her, but more importantly, Alison trusts her."

"I'm going to be Dr. Jekyll and Mr. Hyde," Peter said proudly. "My character will magically change anytime someone makes fun of me. It'll scare the living shit out of them."

Everyone laughed, finding the idea genius. The sound of a car engine drew the group's attention to the front of the school as a green Mustang drove up and parked out front. Emma's eyes got wide, and she sat up in her seat.

"That's Leira Berens," Emma said excitedly.

"And Yumfuck!" Aya shouted.

Leira climbed out of the car, a three-foot-tall Yumfuck jumping out to stand by her side. He wore a red cape with the words *Troll Day* stitched onto the back. Leira had come there to visit her grandmother after hearing about all the dark magic happenings that had gone on near the school in recent days. The kids were thrilled. They loved being around Yumfuck.

The loudspeaker buzzed, and Mara's excited voice came over it. "Attention, all students, we have a break in the plans. Please report to the cafeteria for Troll Day! My granddaughter Leira and Yumfuck Tiberius Troll are walking in as we speak. Refreshments and snacks will be served at each table."

"Snacks," Yumfuck trilled, turning around and waving at all the students.

"This is always strange to me." Luke shook his head.

"Right, a troll with a green tuft is strange, but a man turning into a wolf is perfectly normal," Ethan replied raising an eyebrow.

"I see your point." Luke chuckled, glancing at Izzie with a smile.

Everyone made their way into the cafeteria and sat at their normal tables. Trays of donuts, cakes, cookies, and chips popped up in the center of each, the plates in front of each person shaped like Yumfuck giving a thumbs-up. Alison and Tanner sat next to each other and Alison looked at Leira's soul, recognizing it from the speech during her first year. Next to her was a swirling, whirling wild spray of energy that belonged to the three-foot tall wise one.

Yumfuck jumped up on the podium stationed behind a long table of snacks and put his paws in the air. Everyone in the cafeteria cheered loudly, getting to their feet and giving him the welcome they all thought he deserved. Phones snapped pictures of the furry little guy wearing cowboy boots and a red cape. He patted the air with his little paws and waited for the crowd to quiet.

Mara walked over and clicked on a mic, handing it to Yumfuck with a smile. "Aloha!"

He turned to the group and smiled before letting his face fall to a serious expression as the students sat back down. "Students of the School of Necessary Magic, I am Yumfuck Tiberius Troll. If you haven't met me before, you have met me now."

The freshmen whispered to each other. They'd heard the stories of both Leira and the troll but had never imagined they would get to meet them. Yumfuck held his paw up and quieted the crowd once again.

"I love this time of year. It's my favorite season, and Halloween is my favorite holiday. One day a year, for twenty-four hours, the veil between the World in Between and this world gets so thin it's possible for some to see and hear those they love. My grandmother, your headmistress, has been to the depths of the World in Between, and she came back stronger and brighter than ever. If you ever find yourself wondering about her powers, just know she did what very few have ever been able to do: returned from the realm that lasts for an eternity."

The students got to their feet and cheered again, this time in recognition of Mara. She waved her hand at the students and laughed, finding herself suddenly the center of attention. When the students sat back down Yumfuck removed his cape and handed it to Leira, who shoved it into her pocket.

"I hope that everyone has a very Happy Halloween, and don't forget to look out for the things that go bump in the night!"

He chortled and put his paw over his head, jumped from the podium, shrinking in midair to just five inches, and cannonballed into a large bowl of cheese puffs. He chomped down as he swam through, and flipped over to do the backstroke. Orange dust covered his fur, but no one cared. They all thought he was the most amazing thing they had ever seen. Leira rolled her eyes and laughed at the theatrics, realizing that minus the speech, he pretty much did the same thing at home.

Mara leaned into Leira and nudged her. "Things never change, do they?"

"Nope, but I have to tell you, I am starting to like that fact. Let's just hope we don't encourage anyone here to go get a troll. You don't need one running around the schoolhouse."

"No, indeed." She sighed. "I have enough on my plate between normal teen angst and the dark magic issues in the area. I don't need a wild troll running all over the school diving into people's ice cream bowls when they aren't looking."

Yumfuck jumped out of the bowl and shook his fur, a haze of cheese dust floating off him and up toward the ceiling. He jumped to the floor and put his hands on his hips, tapping his foot to whatever beat was in his head. The kids watched as he slowly grew taller and taller, reaching his max height of eight feet. His tuft of green fur reached the ceiling. He trilled at the applause and shrank back down to four feet, rolling his shoulders and cracking his knuckles.

"Uh oh, he's about to really show off." Mara laughed. "I missed you guys so much. Every time I went to the grocery store and passed the junk food aisle I was sad. I actually was excited yesterday to blow money on all this junk, knowing it would be necessary for Yumfuck's survival at the school."

"It's his annoyance fuel. The more jacked up he is, the more he will show off." Leira laughed.

"Good. It'll keep the students in here and out of trouble."

A cheer went up as Yumfuck spun in a circle so fast all that you saw was the swirl of his fur. When he stopped he had morphed into a terrier, his tuft of green hair still there and his sharp little chompers visible through his grin. The kids clapped every time he changed. He went through the list of animals—a pony, a green-haired giraffe, a large bear, and even one of the giant elk from the Oriceran forests. He was a regular showstopper.

Mara walked over and grabbed the mic, putting her

hand up. "Just a warning. I know he is fun, but please steer clear of trolls. They bond for life, and by life, I mean they go everywhere you go, causing a streak of problems behind them."

Yumfuck frowned at her, and she shook her head. "Not now, Yumfuck. You are now the defender of the innocent, but you can't deny that your first trip around the sun was a doozie with stolen donuts, terrified criminals, and a movie theatre that was shut down because they thought they had an infestation of rats."

Yumfuck chuckled and nodded. "She's right. We *are* mischievous."

He grew to six feet and dropped to all fours, his body quickly morphing into a very large lion. He let out a loud roar, his green tuft laid over to the side as his mane. Everyone cheered again while they stuffed their faces with junk food.

"What are you going to be for Halloween, Yumfuck?" one of the students yelled.

"Oh, young Padawan." He smiled, morphing from the lion into a shorter and hairier version of Yoda. He looked at Leira, who jumped and grabbed a jacket out of her back pocket, tossing it to him. It was a kid's karate jacket he had gotten from a consignment shop, but when he put it on he closely resembled a hairy version of Yoda.

"Fun if you don't get sliced by the man who breathes way too heavy, Halloween will be. Feel the force!"

Everyone laughed and cheered as he morphed back into himself and started to go table to table, talking to all the students. Kathleen turned around with a smile on her face, surprising everyone. She looked at them and shrugged.

"I don't want one or anything, but I can't deny the dang guy is completely adorable."

"My great grandfather accidentally saved one when he was a kid." Emma sighed. "The thing turned out to be his best friend, and when he died, his troll peacefully died as well. They were celebrated together during the Oriceran funeral procession. It was the only time I got to see the customs of Oriceran."

"That's neat." Aya smiled. "I mean, not your grandfather dying, but... You know what I mean."

Emma giggled and rubbed her shoulder. "You should get a troll. You two can be awkward together."

20

That night, after everyone had crashed for an afternoon nap from all the junk food they ate, Horace went out into the field and started a huge bonfire, probably the biggest any of the kids had ever seen. Mara Berens, of course, made sure to put a protective barrier around it to keep anyone from getting hurt, but it was really something to see. Many of the students stood close to it with long sticks, melting marshmallows to make s'mores. Yumfuck hummed as he walked around, looking like Yoda holding a bag of marshmallows. Every few steps he tossed one up in the air and caught it with his mouth, munching happily.

In the courtyard, students took turns carving jack-o-lanterns. Some wanted to do it the old-fashioned way, scooping out the guts and using a jigsaw knife to carve scary faces into the pumpkins. Others got more creative and used their wands to etch intricate swirling designs into the pumpkin skin. Four of the upperclassmen walked around and collected the bowls of guts. They separated the seeds and used magic to fry them in butter on the small outside stationary grill. Every time a batch was done they poured them into bowls. There were so many that they overflowed onto one of the tables.

Kathleen walked up to the table to carve one the old-fashioned way, but she looked at her furry arms and long sphinx claws and decided she didn't want to walk around for the rest of the night with pumpkin guts crusted in her fur. She pulled out her wand and swirled it around, cutting a floral print around the stem and using her magic to scoop out the guts and put them in a bowl. She then carved a selfie of her as a sphinx into the pumpkin and used an orb of light to make it glow.

Horace stood to the side with his arms folded, watching proudly as pumpkins covered the porch and the court-yard's lawn.

"You did a good job growing the pumpkins this year." Mara smiled and jabbed her elbow into his side. "I'm still wondering what you did with that enormous one that was bigger than your cottage."

He smiled. "You'll see later.

"I can't wait. I love surprises."

Leira smiled and nodded at Horace as she followed her grandmother around the grounds, keeping one eye on Yumfuck to make sure he wasn't causing any mischief. He was having a blast. He played with all the kids, recited lines from *Star Wars* with the guys, and snuck up on Kathleen to pet her soft sphinx fur, which scared the crap out of her. Everyone thought it was hilarious; even Kathleen, who grabbed Yumfuck and squeezed him.

Alison loved sitting near the warmth of the fire, watching the excitement flow through the souls of her classmates. Tanner sat down beside her, magic energy floating all over him.

"I'm a pirate. A real one, at least for the night."

"Don't make me walk the plank." She giggled.

"You look beautiful by the way, and it looks like you are a girl pirate."

"Izzie spilled the beans, so I thought why not?"

"I love it " He laughed, kissing her cheek and taking her hand in his.

Across the courtyard, Grace sat with Scarlett and Wyatt talking happily about the costumes. For once Scarlett was actually being nice. She'd even complimented some of the freshmen on their clothes. Wyatt had chilled out and was just enjoying the night air. Grace didn't usually hang out with them since she didn't like Scarlett's friends too much, but when it was just the three of them, Scarlett let go of her insecurities and was just herself. Deep down she was a pretty decent person, surprisingly.

"I can't wait for the fireworks." Scarlett smiled. "Horace may be a human, but put him and the headmistress together and they put on one hell of a show."

"Oh, yeah." Wyatt nodded, popping a handful of pumpkin seeds into his mouth. "I remember last year's. Horace did the backgrounds really well, and Mara shot those moving ones from her wand. That one dragon one at the end almost scared the pants off the new kids."

Grace laughed loudly. "Yeah, it swooped down like it was going to eat them, and then exploded into little sparkling falling stars. That was great."

Grace looked around while listening to them talk about the different fireworks shows they'd seen since they'd started attending the school. She grabbed a handful of seeds and lifted her hand to her mouth, but stopped before she could toss them in. Slowly she lowered her hand to the table and stared at the edge of the garden. Standing under a large oak was a wispy image of her long-dead and very beloved grandmother.

She sat there staring for a moment, unsure if it was real or if someone was playing a really mean trick on her. Her grandmother lifted her semi-translucent arm and blew into her palm. Sparkling dust floated over the heads of the other students and pushed into Grace's chest. She took a deep breath, feeling the warmth of the energy, and her tears filled her eyes.

She jumped up and ran for the garden, and her grandmother's image disappeared around the corner. Scarlett looked at Wyatt, not sure if they had both seen the same thing.

"Did you see a ghost?"

"Uh, yeah," Wyatt replied.

"We need to stop her."

Scarlett and Wyatt jumped up and bolted after her, calling her name to try to stop her. By that point Grace was already almost to the garden, and they slowed down, panting, and watched her disappear into the shadows. Their friends from around the bonfire called their names, and Scarlett looked at Wyatt and shrugged.

"Guess she gets to hang out with an old lady tonight."

Wyatt nodded. "Guess so. Come on, let's make some s'mores."

They joined their friends, giving it only one more thought before focusing on the festivities. Leira stood to the side watching the whole thing unravel. She'd seen the apparition and the stream of energy hit the girl. She knew that this was the night for ghosts from the World in Between to make a showing, but she also knew it wasn't limited to the good ones. The bad ones could do it also, tricking unsuspecting magical beings back into the void with them.

She reached down and grabbed Yumfuck's shoulder before he could run off again. He turned and looked at her curiously, following her line of sight to the gardens.

"A girl just chased a ghost into the gardens. I need you to follow. Make sure she is okay, and there is no dark magic trying to trick her into the void."

Yumfuck morphed back into his troll self and grew to four feet tall. He scurried through the kids and slowed down as he cautiously entered the gardens. He followed the dimly lit path to the center, where he saw Grace staring at her grandmother's image with tears running down her cheeks.

"Grandma," she said, putting her hand out.

"That's close enough," she whispered. "I am in a place that you cannot enter."

"The World in Between?"

"Yes, and tonight I was able to figure out how to show myself to you.'

"I should get someone…the headmistress maybe, to try to get you out," she said in a panicked tone.

"No." Her grandmother smiled. "It won't work; not here, not now. I wanted to come to you and tell you that I am always with you, even if you can't see me. I sneak off to different places and watch almost every day. You have grown into such a beautiful and wonderful woman, Grace. I am so proud of you."

"Oh, Grandma, I miss you so much," she sobbed.

"I know, but now you know that I am not far away. I am right beside you almost all the time. I'm sorry I left so suddenly, I didn't plan it, but I knew you were strong and wise, and that you would make good choices and be the magical being I knew you could be."

Her grandmother looked over her shoulder at something behind her that Grace couldn't see. She took a deep breath and fought to keep the worry from her face.

"I'm out of time, Grace."

"No," she cried.

"Know that I love you and that I am always watching out for you. Be strong, sweetheart."

"I love you too, Grandma. Try to come back and see me."

"You know I'll do my best."

Leira came jogging up to Yumfuck and knelt, watching as Grace said a tear-filled goodbye to her grandmother. It pulled at Leira's heart, remembering how many times she wished she could see Mara, not knowing where she had gone or if she would ever see her again. Leira put her hand on Yumfuck's shoulder and nodded.

"I know what that is like. Give her a moment to say a proper goodbye."

Yumfuck nodded with a solemn look on his face, his paws crossed in front of him. They tried not to eavesdrop, but at the same time, they needed to keep a close eye on the girl. The veil between the worlds was thin, and anything could happen.

Grace wiped a tear from her cheek and stepped forward as her grandmother's apparition wavered and began to fade. Suddenly there was a loud tearing noise, and a rip opened right in front of Grace. Leira looked up with wide eyes as Grace began to lose her footing. Her arms windmilled wildly as she tried to pull back.

Yumfuck sprinted for her, growing in size with every step. He scooped Grace up as he ran past and dove out the way, rolling into one of the flower beds. He opened his arms and found Grace safe and sound, with tears flowing down her cheeks. He set her down and shrunk back to three feet, reaching up and taking her hand.

Leira jumped in front of the rift, grimacing at the goop that seeped out onto the grass and killed everything it touched. She pulled the energy from the ground, feeling the tingle of her bracelet on her wrist. The magic swirled up through her chest and down her arms, bursting in a steady stream from her palms. As it struck the rift, she heard the screeching of some sort of creature from the other side.

Finally, the rift slammed shut, and the air cleared as if nothing had ever happened. Leira let out a deep breath, walked over to Grace, and grasped her arms. She looked at her puffy red eyes and smiled comfortingly.

"Are you all right?"

She nodded her head, sniffling.

"You've been through quite a lot, and I know how it feels to see a loved one like that. At least you know she is watching you."

"What...what was that? I could hear screaming and growling."

"That was a rift. It split open because the veil was so thin. Your grandmother found a way to communicate, and the creatures used that to try to grab you and pull you inside."

"Is she okay?"

Leira really didn't know the answer to that, but she saw the pleading in the young girl's eyes. It reminded her of herself when she was younger—before all the magic had hit—when she was trying desperately to find answers and maintain hope.

Leira smiled and nodded. "I'm sure she will be okay. Come on, let's get you cleaned up."

21

General Anderson sat in the back of the town car as he drove out of the city of Charlottesville and through the countryside. He'd always liked it out there; it was beautiful, especially this time of year. The fields were still green, but the trees were losing the last of their vivid fall leaves. Whenever the government demanded he visit, he made sure he did it before winter hit. He never was one for the Virginia snowfall. It was too bitter and frozen for him, and the summers weren't a prime time to come either.

He stared out at the rolling hills, the large southern mansions perched up high with the bright morning sunshine shimmering down on them. He hadn't told Mara Berens he was coming and felt kind of bad for just dropping in like that, even though that was the entire point of surprise inspections. He knew his presence made everyone nervous, but he also knew Mara Berens had run a tight ship for years. He was impressed by the way she had handled the issue with the student who had been hexed the year before, but that was what had prompted the government to call for an inspection. That, and their new ROTC/MD program that no one seemed to care about.

Then again, after the latest debacle with secret agents going into the resort kemana to spy and find out how humans could take them over, he completely understood why they might not be so keen to trust humans with anything, especially magical warfare. Still, it was his country, and he was charged with maintaining the connection between the two worlds. He had to admit, though, he was close to wanting to take that retirement and sleep for about a week straight.

After hemming and hawing over it, he picked up his cell and called Mara.

"This is Mara Berens."

"Mara, it's General Anderson. How are you today?"

"I'm well, General. How may I help you?"

"I didn't just want to show up and knock. I am about fifteen minutes out for a surprise inspection."

He could hear the quaver in Mara's voice. "Oh, how lovely."

"I hope you didn't have anything stressful planned today."

"Nope, not at all. It's the weekend, so most of the students are out and about. It's a perfect day to drop in...unannounced."

"Good, I'm glad to hear it. I'll see you soon."

"Perfect."

He ended the call and tossed the phone on the seat next to him, chuckling at the panic in her voice. She did that every time, and even when he showed up with no warning at all, the school was perfectly fine. He could still remember the one time he had shown up mid-day when classes were in session, and kids were running around everywhere. Her face had been priceless when she turned the corner and saw him standing in the foyer. Sometimes she forgot he knew they were teenagers, and with magical ones, anything was possible.

Mara hung up and set the phone on her desk, taking a surreal moment to process what was just said. She started to laugh, not because anything was funny but because everything was very not funny. She had just spent a good four hours on the phone with Grace's parents, trying to explain what had happened when their daughter had nearly been sucked into the World in Between during a Halloween celebration on the grounds of the school. Grace was fine, but her parents? Not so much. They were thankful to Leira but didn't understand how she'd gotten into that position.

Finally, after Grace got on the phone and told her parents about seeing and talking with her grandmother and where she was they calmed down, but were very emotional about the message she'd gotten. They understood how Grace could have slipped away, and how she could have been drawn in after missing her grandmother for so many years. It helped that Mara had given her perspective too, having been on the other side. Not that she told them all the bad stuff; just the part where she'd watched Leira from different places where the veil was thin. It comforted them, especially since Mara had escaped, but she didn't have high hopes for Grace's grandmother.

She lifted her head and took a deep breath as Izzie poked her head around the corner of the office.

"Izzie, perfect timing. Come in."

"Okay," Izzie replied, looking at her suspiciously. "You're not going to put me to work, are you?"

"No, quite the opposite, actually. I am giving you and your friends day passes to go to the kemana and explore. My only stipulation is that it is not negotiable. You all have to go, and I want you to do it in the next ten minutes."

"Uh, okay, sure." Izzie was completely shocked, but she wasn't going to ask why. She didn't want to jinx it. She hadn't asked up to that point because she figured Mara would tell her no, having kept a close watch on her since the year before.

Mara pulled out a pad of paper and quickly started writing the passes for each of them. "So that's Luke, Tanner, Ethan, Peter, Kathleen, Aya, Emma, you, and Alison, correct?"

"You really know my friends." Izzie laughed.

Mara smiled and handed over the passes. "I know my students."

Just then there was a loud knock on the front door, the sound echoing down the hall. Izzie looked over her shoulder. "Who is that? No one knocks."

"Some people knock." Mara sighed. "And don't you worry about it. Go gather your hooligans and get out of here. I have a meeting—an important one—and I'd rather not have any students lurking around pulling pranks or accidentally setting off waves of energy because their emotions get the best of them."

"You don't have to tell me twice." Izzie smiled. "Good luck!"

"As you can see, General, we have made some general maintenance changes to the house, but all in all we've kept it very similar to what it was when it was first opened. And of course, pretty much the same as it was the last time that you took an unexpected tour of the place."

"Yes, everything seems to be very much in order. Let me ask you...did you ever figure out who was behind that young boy's curse?"

Mara sighed. "We found the first toombie, but we are sure there are others."

"Toombie," he repeated quietly. "The orphans injected with dark magic when they are young."

"Yes, sir."

"And have you found the rest of the orphans in the school?"

"We know who they are, and we are watching them very closely."

"But they are still free to attend classes and such?"

Mara looked at the general, trying to keep her composure. "I'm sorry, General, but I was not aware that we had begun incarcerating young children simply on the grounds of where they grew up."

The general shook his head, realizing what it sounded

like he was implying. "Uh, no, of course not. That would be barbaric, and not in anyone's best interests."

"I agree. Besides, if one of them is a toombie they will have no idea, and it really doesn't matter where you lock them up. When the switch is thrown, their magic will get out. I would rather it be in an atmosphere where we can attempt to counteract it than tucked away in a cell."

"Yes." He nodded, suddenly feeling uncomfortable.

Mara smiled and put her hand out, gesturing to the cafeteria. "Where they eat their meals."

"Do you still have the magic plates? That was always so neat to me, and I'm pretty sure my wife would feel the same."

"We do, and if you'd like, we can have lunch here."

"No, unfortunately, I am not going to be able to stay that long. I have several meetings, on the plane and back in the office. But another time."

"Of course."

Mara turned to walk out of the cafeteria, spotting the ROTC board across the way. She waved her hand in front of her, and the virtual screen went blank. They walked into the entryway, and she watched as he happily glanced at the signups for the different clubs and plays.

"Is there a board for the ROTC/MD?"

"Well, we thought it was much too important for a bulletin board and paper sign-up sheet, so we discuss the idea during during first period with everyone."

"Nice. And how are things progressing? The government put a lot of time, effort, and, of course, money into creating this program. We are looking for the best and brightest, starting here in high school, moving forward to college, and then on to the active service—serving the magical community of course."

"Oh, of course. You know, with any new venture it takes time to really pique their interest," Mara replied, downplaying the fact that no one gave two shits about the program. "Teenagers these days, with their technology and such. Always on the move, always distracted by one thing or another. We will continue to pump the information to them, of course, making it sound just as splendid as it is."

He smiled and nodded, his hand tucked between the top two buttons of his dress uniform jacket. "Very good, Ms. Berens. As always, I will have nothing but good things to report."

"Fantastic." Mara smiled, showing him to the door of the mansion. "Please stop by any time."

"I will do so when I can."

Mara stood at the door and watched as the general's guards escorted him from the building to the car parked out front. He waved as he got in and Mara gave her best political grin, waving back. When the car pulled away, she shut the large wooden doors and leaned her head back against them. She shook her head back and forth, so glad the meeting had been a success. It had the potential to have been a complete disaster, and she knew that.

She walked back past the ROTC/MD board and flicked her wrist. The virtual screen came back on with an American and Oriceran flag flying in the background next to one another. She scoffed, letting out a loud laugh.

"ROTC, Magical Division," she grumbled. "Yeah, right. Magical beings don't trust humans as far as they can throw them, in general."

Mara was sure that the general knew this, or at least had some idea that it was true. If he *didn't* know, she wasn't going to be the one who spilled the beans. It was much easier to let him think they were all supportive of the government, especially when the government was the one funding the school.

It was a constant work in progress, and Mara didn't see that going away any time soon. The magical community was only going to grow larger, and she knew that in time kids would sign up for the program, but for now, they didn't even know if they could trust the magicals working with the government. It was a sore spot, and Mara heard it all the time from Leira. She had put her foot down long ago, but the government did things the way they saw fit, even if it meant not including some of the brightest minds in the magical community.

She took off her dress jacket and laid it over the back of one of her office chairs and sat down behind her desk, letting out a deep breath. The school was incredibly quiet, but she had sent pretty much everyone off to the kemana, and the freshmen who stayed behind liked to stay in their dorms. Mara didn't know what the future would bring, but she did know that to have one, they needed to find out who was behind all the dark magic that had been affecting the students lately.

22

"So, let me get this straight. Headmistress Berens pretty much ordered us to go have fun in the kemana?" Ethan asked as they walked slowly down the dark steps to the underground city.

"Yeah, that's what happened." Izzie shrugged.

"And she didn't say why?"

"Nope. Like I said, I dipped my head in to tell her we were going to get lunch, and she called me in and just started writing passes for everyone. Then she basically shooed me out of the room just as a loud knock came on the door."

"Did she say who it was?" Kathleen asked.

"No, but she was kind of sweating and seemed a bit nervous, which is very unlike her from what I have seen of her for the last year and a half."

"I wonder if she had a date?" Emma giggled.

"With whom?" Izzie grimaced. "She spends all her time

here or chasing down dark wizards in town. When does she have time for dating?"

"Maybe it's one of those online websites." Peter chuckled.

"Or maybe...it was Mr. Regency." Aya laughed.

"Oh, God." Izzie grimaced. "Can you imagine the two of them dating?"

"I'd rather not." Ethan scoffed.

"He would have to stand on her desk to kiss her," Kathleen bellowed, her voice echoing down into the dark.

"I would be careful. I know two unsuspecting upperclassmen who still have random bouts of jock itch for making fun of Regency's height," Luke pointed out.

"Yeah, well, I don't have a jock to itch," Kathleen replied. "And I'm pretty sure the other way around would be against some sort of code of conduct."

"Seriously, guys." Ethan stopped at the bottom of the stairs. "Can we just go the whole rest of our day not thinking about Mara Berens dating or saying the words 'jock itch?' Besides, who cares what the reasoning was? We are here."

The group walked out of the doorway, Alison and Tanner bringing up the rear. They all looked around in wonder for a few moments, then wrinkled their noses, remembering the last time they were there together.

"Hey, none of that," Ethan demanded. "This will not be like last time. Come on, let's go over to that general store and exchange our money."

"NO!" Alison and Izzie yelled at the same time, forcing everyone to turn around and stare at them.

Izzie chuckled, walking over and squeezing Alison's

hand and laughing nervously. "That is, the owner there charges more than the other places."

"I heard he went to jail," Tanner revealed. "Something about finding two students from the college tied up in his basement for stealing. Apparently, he was torturing magical beings instead of calling the authorities. Crazy business. The place is probably shut down and boarded up at this point."

Alison lifted an eyebrow and looked over, sensing the nerves in Izzie's energy. Tanner waved to everyone, grabbing Alison's other hand tightly.

"Come on, the café has an exchange at the back. We can get some Ruby Falls there. Plus, they make the best hot chocolate I have ever had."

Alison smiled as they walked toward the large cup of coffee magically steaming next to the café's sign. "How do you know so much about the kemana?"

"You don't think I came to a new school last year and didn't check out the kemana beforehand, did you? I knew it was off limits to freshmen, and I wanted to get a good look. See what this town had to offer."

"Well, that's just awesome. You can help us get around. We've only been here once, and let's just say it didn't go as scheduled."

"That doesn't sound good," Tanner replied.

"Could have been worse." She smiled, gripping his hand tighter as they entered the café.

They made their way to the back where a Crystal was standing behind a counter that looked like it was from one of the humans' banks. Above the window was a large wooden sign engraved with the word Exchange. The group took turns getting their money switched over and waited for Alison and Tanner to finish. Deciding to take Tanner's word for it, they got in line, each ordering a small hot chocolate.

As they walked out of the café Kathleen took a huge sip, getting the mound of whip cream all over her mouth and nose. "Mmm, this really is the best hot chocolate ever."

Emma handed her a napkin and giggled, happy to see her loosen up. As they walked down the street, they looked around at all the different creatures shopping, talking, and making their various ways through the city. Alison watched the energies surrounding them, remembering how many dark souls had been down here when they rescued the boy from the Kilomea. Things weren't so bad this time around, and she was glad because she'd had enough of dark magic for the year.

"Oh, I have to go in here," Kathleen gasped. "I bought a sundress here last year and loved it. I hear their winter gear is even better."

Kathleen ran off, and the rest of the group shrugged and split off. Luke, Izzie, Tanner, and Alison stuck together, while Emma, Ethan, and Peter spotted the local technology store. Aya trailed after Kathleen, not wanting to leave her alone. They shopped and talked for several hours, finally meeting back up, mostly by chance, in the town's square. Kathleen sat down on the edge of the large fountain filled with bubbles and set her six bags down next to her.

"Shopping can be exhausting." Kathleen sighed.

"Oh, I wanted to go to this joke shop I heard about

down here, but it's kind of off the beaten path," Ethan said excitedly. "Why don't we go as a group?"

Everyone shrugged and nodded, figuring that for something of that nature, Ethan would already know how to get there. However, after about forty minutes of weaving through the back streets and finding themselves in a bad neighborhood, everyone was pretty sure that Ethan was completely lost.

"How did you get us here?" Kathleen scoffed, looking around her nervously. "I thought we were going to stay pretty centered in town this time."

"It's not like I got us lost on purpose." Ethan was irritated and tired. "I swear this is where they said it was."

"Obviously not." Emma smiled kindly. "Let's just go back the way we came and get back to the center of town. We can ask someone there. I'm sure they know how to get to it."

The group agreed. Alison clutched Tanner's arm, no longer seeing the streams of souls and energy she had before. She knew they were in a residential area from the small amounts of energy the trees and grass gave off, but other than that she didn't see anything. She'd been so excited just to be walking around with Tanner that she hadn't even thought about sensing where they were going.

"Uh, does anyone know where we came from?" Aya asked.

"Great! We come to the kemana and get lost, and now we can't find our way back to the center. I knew this was a disaster waiting to happen." Kathleen grimaced.

"Can you just chill out?" Ethan barked.

"Guys," Alison called, putting her hands up. "No need to

get angry at each other. We have to stay together. Now, Izzie, why don't you look for magical footprints so we can see what direction the most traffic goes and follow that?"

"Excellent idea." Izzie nodded and pushed up her sleeves.

She closed her eyes and pulled in energy, letting it stream out of the palms of her hands and dissipate over the sidewalk in front of her. She opened her eyes and lifted an eyebrow, turning in a circle. The others glanced at each other and waited for her to say something.

"There are no magical trails but ours," Izzie said. "Like, *none*."

"That's ridiculous. Maybe you are doing it wrong," Kathleen replied. "Only magicals are allowed to live here, so there must be some sort of transportation that gets them around."

Alison let out a deep breath and repeated exactly what Izzie had just done, nodding at the others. There were no others trails to be seen. "Izzie is right There's nothing. Maybe the kemana keeps you from using specific types of magic or something."

They stood there for quite a while, trying not to argue over which direction they needed to go. Finally, a Willen walked out of the house across the street. At first, he panicked, thinking about running from them after assuming they were there for him, but when the sun reflected off a shining bracelet on Kathleen's arm, he pulled down his vest, determined to get it for his wife.

"Hello there," the Willen said, tipping his hat. "You look lost."

"You think?" Ethan growled, pacing back and forth.

Izzie shot him a nasty glance and smiled at the Willen. "I'm Izzie."

"Thomas." He smiled.

"We are lost, and we would really appreciate it if you could show us the way back to town."

"Of course, but Willen never work for free."

"Right." Izzie nodded and pulled out her coin pouch. "How much?"

"I am seeking something other than coins."

"Okay, what?"

The Willen looked at Kathleen's bracelet and cleared his throat. Kathleen looked down at the cuff, sighing and rolling her eyes. She took it off and held it in front of Thomas, but snatched it back as he reached for it.

"Fine, but you better show us all the way back to the center of town, or you will be pulling this bracelet out of places where the sun don't shine."

Thomas swallowed hard and nodded, taking the bracelet and chuckling excitedly as he placed it in the pouch hanging from his vest. "My wife will love it. Now, follow close and keep up."

With as small a price the Willen asked for the group half-expected to turn the corner and be there, but they had gravely underestimated how far into the kemana Ethan had led them. When they finally reached the town square, they were relieved and exhausted. The Willen put his paws out and smiled widely.

"Tada!"

Izzie smiled and patted him on the head. "Thanks, Thomas. It was a pleasure meeting you."

"You too, Izzie, and you guys be safe getting back to school."

They all took a moment to thank him before deciding that everything else they did in the kemana would be strictly in the center and that they were going to stick together. They stopped into the local candy store, then went into an old bookstore where Peter purchased a skull and an old spell book.

Alison walked out of the shop and tripped over a Crystal's long slippery icicles.

"Watch out," he barked, narrowing his eyes for a moment at Alison as if there was something about her that he recognized.

"Oh...sorry," Alison replied, hurrying toward Tanner and grabbing his hand.

"You'd better be," he growled under his breath, heading past them toward the residential area.

"Friendly lot around here." Ethan sighed. "Anyway, I don't know about you guys, but I'm pretty happy with the stuff I found. I'm ready to head back. We can have dinner in the cafeteria and try to sneak a peek at Mara's new boyfriend."

Everyone agreed on the going back part. They'd noticed that the later in the day it got, the shiftier the crowd of magic beings on the street became. They wanted to end the trip before they jinxed themselves like the first time, and the longer they stayed, the more likely they would find trouble.

23

By the time everyone had exited the stairs from the kemana and the evening sun hit their faces, all was forgiven and Ethan was in a better mood. Emma, Peter, and Aya walked ahead of everyone, anxious to get to the dining hall. They'd decided not to eat in the kemana because it was a waste of money, so now they were starving. Ethan jogged up next to Kathleen and handed her a gift shop bag. She looked at him out of the corner of her eye and took it, pulling a gold cuff from the bag. It was just like the one she had given the Willen.

"When did you get this?"

"While you guys were in the candy shop. I figured I owed you. You paid for us to get back after I got us completely lost."

Kathleen smiled. "Thanks, Ethan. I appreciate you noticing."

"No problem." He grinned, hurrying past to catch up with Peter.

Izzie bumped her hip into Kathleen's and smiled at her as she looked at the cuff. Kathleen didn't say anything, but Izzie could tell she was happy to be acknowledged for giving up her bracelet. To be honest, Kathleen had been a bit bummed about it since it had been a gift from her father, but she would cherish the new one the same, if not more.

The group trekked along the side of the mansion and out into the courtyard. Luke walked happily next to Izzie.

"Luke," Max Regency called, waving his hand.

"I'll wait here." Izzie smiled.

Luke jogged over to the coach, his stomach churning. "Luke, I'm glad I found you. I wanted to let you know that you made the Louper team. You won't be first-string, at least not right away, but you definitely showed me that you are one hell of a player. Next semester will begin the season, and in the meantime, I will work on some of the things I think you could use to improve your skills."

"Really?" Luke exclaimed. "Thank you so much, coach. I promise I won't let you down. I've been dreaming about being on a Louper team since I first saw the game. I've been practicing my butt off, and have already read the books you suggested during tryouts."

"You have?" Max was impressed. None of his other students had listened to what he was saying, much less volunteered to do more work.

"I liked them, and I ended up buying a copy of each so I could highlight the beginner advice and tactics."

"Good. They really do help. Now, run along. The rest of the team already knows who is playing with them, and you were the last to tell."

Luke smiled and ran over to Izzie, grabbing her around the waist and twirling around.

"Wow, what in the world?"

"I made the team!"

"That is so amazing!" Izzie wrapped her arms around him and squeezed.

"Come on, let's go tell the others."

As soon as they walked into the cafeteria the older boys who made the team met Luke at the door, pushing Izzie to the side and patting him on the back. Izzie smiled and walked over to the table, sitting down with the others.

"Congrats, dude. We are really stoked to have you on the team."

"Thanks, guys." Luke actually felt like a person for once, not the shifter everyone constantly picked on.

"Come on. You can sit with us now at meals. We all stay together."

Luke paused, looking at the group—the people who were truly his friends—and didn't know what to say. He wanted to be part of the team, but at the same time, he didn't want to make his friends think he had moved on from them. If it weren't for them, he might not have had the courage to even try out for the team.

Izzie forced a smile and looked at everyone at the table. "He made the Louper team."

"Awesome," Peter replied.

They all turned and looked at Luke, wondering if he was going to sit with the team or come sit with them. They had accepted Luke when no one else would give him the time of day, and were a little shocked that he was struggling to make the choice. Izzie had mixed emotions about it. She knew how badly he wanted to be on the team and fit in with people, but she still couldn't help but feel like he was moving on.

Ethan waved to him, but he just looked like a deer in headlights. "Well, apparently our usefulness has worn out."

"Let him enjoy his celebration. Sheesh," Kathleen responded, turning back around to read a magazine as she ate her chicken breast and brown rice.

No one said a thing, they just watched. After a few minutes, Luke finally decided to go with the jocks. The decision really didn't shock any of the group, and they tried to act like they didn't care. In truth, everyone but Kathleen felt a little jilted. Even Tanner, who hadn't spent that much time with Luke.

Izzie watched as her plate filled with Fettucine Alfredo and looked up at Peter, smiling. "Have you come up with any new spells lately?"

"A couple of minor ones, and I am still tweaking the room-cleaning one."

"We need that one when you get it all down." Kathleen chuckled. "We aren't messy, but none of us enjoys cleaning, that's for sure."

"Be careful with that one, or you might end up with an even messier room and no eyebrows." Ethan laughed.

"I told you I fixed it, and it wasn't an entire eyebrow, just a swipe through the middle."

"You looked like Vanilla Ice's smaller and way less hip brother."

Everyone burst into laughter, picturing Peter dancing and wearing harem pants and boots. The table tried to move on; tried to let go of the fact that their friend had chosen people who had hated him two days before but were suddenly his best friends because of some game. The sound of the laughter carried to Luke and from time to time he would look at them, ignoring the banter between the jocks. All they talked about were trophies and game strategies, and Luke already missed the jokes with his friends.

Ethan glanced at Luke and frowned again. Izzie shook her head.

"We should be getting on with things, not sending Luke death stares across the hall. Seriously, you two were some of his big supporters, and he got exactly what you hoped for."

"Yeah, and now we are chopped liver," Ethan mumbled.

"Luke is still our friend, and he is still the guy we were with in the kemana an hour ago. It might take a little time to get used to, but he doesn't have to be glued to our side or prove anything to us. He is his own person. If we want to be the good friends here, then we need to accept that things might be different at mealtimes and be happy for him. He busted his ass trying to make this team, and now that he has. I won't accept you bullying him over it."

"All right, all right." Ethan chuckled. "You made your point. Let Luke enjoy his victory, even if it's not with us."

Kathleen rolled her eyes. "God, you act like he picked up and moved schools or something. It's one dinner so far. Stop being so sensitive."

"I pride myself on my feminine sensitivity," Ethan joked.

"Right, more like as sensitive as a brick." Kathleen giggled, making everyone else laugh too.

Izzie put on a brave face, but she couldn't help feeling hurt. She was going to take her own advice, though, and support him in whatever made him happy.

That night Alison and Izzie stood by their beds, folding laundry and putting it away. Izzie thought about Luke the whole time, wishing she wasn't being so selfish about it. He was still her friend. That hadn't changed.

"You okay?" Alison asked, sensing the sadness in her friend's energy.

"You can see my mood, can't you?"

"More like your emotions, but yeah. I can tell you are hurt over Luke picking a different table."

"Am I right to be hurt?"

Alison smiled. "You have the right to feel however you feel, but I don't think it would be right to make *him* feel bad about it."

"I wouldn't do that; not unless he totally ditched us and turned into another Wyatt or Henry. Even then I will wish him well and keep my feelings to myself."

"Good. I want you to be happy too, not just him."

Izzie reached over and squeezed Alison's hand. "Thank you."

The rest of the girls filed into the room after their showers. Kathleen took the towel from around her head and pulled out a bottle of gel. The girls watched as she squeezed a glob into her palm and ran it through her hair, scrunching the ends. They were used to seeing Kathleen always ready—straight red hair, not a thread out of place.

Kathleen looked up and smiled at them. "What? Everyone keeps telling me I will really come into my own in high school. I decided that I wanted it to be true, and not just wear or do my hair the way everyone else likes it."

Alison walked toward Kathleen and put her hands out, taking hers. "You will be beautiful to us no matter what."

"As sweet as that is, I'm not sure the blind girl should be the one making judgment calls on my beauty," she joked, wrapping her arms around Alison. "I'm just kidding. Thank you; the words mean so much to me."

Alison smiled and went back over to her bed. She put the last of her laundry away and pulled down the covers. She was actually pretty tired, and she knew that once the girls were asleep, she would have no problem falling into a meditative state. Izzie sighed and climbed into bed, pulling the covers up as Aya clicked off the lights.

"Night, everyone," Izzie called.

"Night," they all responded.

Alison waited until she knew the girls were asleep. They all knew she was a Drow and that she was blind, but she wasn't ready to tell them she really didn't sleep either. They'd probably start to think she was a vampire or something.

As her eyes drifted shut, she focused on her breathing. She replayed the events of the past week, watching everything unfold. When she reached the precise moment where she saw herself in her bed, she opened her eyes. Alison didn't want to get in the habit of looking into the future. It was a dangerous power, and she figured it was best to only use it in case of emergency.

She cleared her mind and rolled onto her side,

watching the shimmers of energy out in the fields. Though she was still tired, she recognized that she needed to meditate in small chunks until she had control of her talents. So instead, she let the energy of the fairies in the distance take her through the night.

24

The next day the girls got up and pulled on their gym wear. The grey and blue t-shirts matched the mesh shorts, and even the socks had the crest of the school on the outside of the calf. They pulled their hair back in pony-tails and headed to breakfast. None of them were thrilled about taking a gym class, but Kathleen was the worst. She had tried to get herself excused, but in the end, she was decked out and ready to play.

"What do you think we will do in gym?" Aya asked as she ate her eggs.

"Probably do wind sprints and some stupid western dance. I feel like no matter how old it gets, every class from now to the Year 3000 will include them."

"I don't know about you guys, but I am not thrilled about doing the honky tonk." Izzie sighed and glanced at Luke, who was sitting with the Louper team.

"I doubt we are doing that." Emma giggled. "I'm sure it won't be too painful. It's only an hour."

When breakfast was over, they headed outside to the soccer field. They lined up as Annabelle Grant came jogging over. Her clothes were the same as the girls', except a slightly messier version. Tripping over her own feet, she stumbled slightly. She blew her hair out of her face and spun the ball in her hands as she looked at the girls.

The girls were surprised that she was the gym teacher. "Morning, ladies. The original gym teacher isn't with us any longer, so I volunteered to take over. There were a lot of interesting things to do in the syllabus, and although I'm a huge fan of line dancing, I decided to start us out with a little dodgeball instead."

Izzie glanced at Kathleen and held back a giggle. She could barely understand how Professor Grant stayed upright when she walked. She couldn't imagine her line dancing without falling down and breaking a leg or something. Professor Grant pulled out her wand and looked at the class.

"Who here has played magical dodgeball before?"

A couple of girls raised their hands, and Professor Grant smiled. "Okay, great. Now, for anyone not familiar with the magical side of the game, this is how it works. Instead of throwing the ball at opposing team members who try to catch it or dodge it, this red rubber ball does all the work. It will hover and bounce and throw itself at different people. The ball doesn't distinguish between teams, so everyone is fair game. I want to warn you that the ball has a mind of its own and once I put the spell on it, I won't have any control over where it goes."

Izzie raised her hand. "So, if the ball is throwing itself, how do you win?"

"That's the fun part. This is an individual game, so no teams. The last one who grabs the ball and holds on as it attempts to buck you off is our winner. So, spread out across the field, and get ready."

The girls jogged to different parts of the field. Alison was nervous about this one. She was definitely at a disadvantage since she didn't yet know if she could see the ball flying at her head. She moved to the back of the field and put her hands on her knees. She scanned the girls, and found Izzie to the left and up the field about twenty yards. Professor Grant waved her wand over the ball before tapping it three times and holding it out in front of her.

The ball flew into the air and stopped. It hovered like it was searching out its first victim. Alison watched as the magical energy attached to the ball struck down three of her teammates. She noticed that every time the energy and magic switched to a new location, the color of the ball changed. It wasn't long before she picked up on what the different colors meant as it sped across the field.

She took a deep breath as the ball flashed green, then orange, as it tried to fake Kathleen out. It shot forward, hitting her on the top of the head and knocked her out of the game. She actually looked relieved to be out. She was not a bug person or a woods person, and now the girls knew that she wasn't a sports kind of girl either.

Aya covered her mouth, trying not to laugh as the ball bounced off Kathleen's head and flew straight up into the air, but before she could get herself under control, the ball hurtled down the field straight at her. Aya's eyes grew wide as it flew straight for her head. At the last second, Aya ducked out of the way. The ball smashed the girl behind her in the stomach, doubling her over and knocking her to her knees.

The ball was vicious, and this seemed more like a punishment than an actual fun game. Even the guys on the other side of the field, who watched and laughed as the girls went down hard, tried not to get hit in the face. The ball wasn't hard by any means, but it stung when it smacked into you. It also flew fast enough to knock you right off your feet.

The only thing that kept them playing was the promise that at least one person that might actually beat it at its own game. The ball was cocky and played with the girls before hitting them. However, with that magical arrogance, it was prone to making mistakes. The remaining girls, including Izzie, Alison, and Emma, squatted low with their hands out in front of them. They were starting to get the feel of things.

They had to catch the ball, but it wasn't like it would just go limp when they caught it. They had to then try to hold onto it for longer than five seconds while it bucked wildly around. The ball was strong enough to pull someone into the air. If they held on for five seconds or more, they won. In the past, others had tried to break the school record of two minutes and seventeen seconds. That record had been on the books for about seven years without anyone even coming close.

All the girls' eyes shone with the determination to try, except for Alison's. She just wanted to end the game without a bloody nose. Professor Grant shot a nervous glance around the field. The last thing she wanted was for one of the girls to get hurt on her first day as the gym teacher. She was clumsy enough for the whole school, constantly wired on coffee and Red Bull as she tried to keep up with her normal classes, and now this.

The ball swerved back and forth in the air above the girl's heads. It was starting to tease them, lurching in one direction and then bolting in another. Izzie licked her lips and danced back and forth as the ball shifted right, then flew full speed toward her. She ducked and pivoted, and it homed in on the girl behind her.

The girl flinched, balling up to take the blow. Izzie dove forward and latched onto the thing just before the ball hit the girl in the stomach. As if it had a mind that could be surprised, the ball shimmied a bit and took off wildly tossing Izzie back and forth, up and down, and side to side. She clutched the ball tightly. She was determined to hit the mark.

The ball swooped low, and Izzie pushed off the ground to land on top of it. Izzie rode it like it was a small bronco as it tried to dislodge her. Professor Grant stared at her watch. When it hit the five-second mark, she blew her whistle loudly. Izzie didn't let go, though. She wanted to hold on as long as she could. She knew that with her lack of sports ability, this opportunity would probably only come once for her.

From Alison's perspective, all she saw was the small shimmer of energy from the ball and Izzie's soul being flung back and forth through the air. Professor Grant held her hand up, and the other girls looked at her anxiously.

"Thirty seconds!" she yelled.

Izzie took in a deep breath and dug her fingers into it even harder as she leaned forward and began to push the ball downward. She struggled as the girls chanted her name. Across the field, the guys had stopped and were lined up watching Izzie go to town. Among them was Luke, and he was pretty impressed by how hard Izzie was hanging onto victory.

"One minute," Professor Grant shouted.

Alison laughed and clapped her hands, cheering Izzie on. "Come on, Izzie, hold tight! You are almost there!"

This continued on until Professor Grant held up her hand again., "Two minutes! Come on, Izzie, hold on eighteen more seconds, and you got the school record."

It never failed that the last few seconds always seemed like the most impossible. Izzie roared as her arms flexed and relaxed with the ball's movement. She swung her legs around and let her feet hit the ground first, catapulting her and the ball high up into the air. As she started to descend Professor Grant called time and shot a stream of white light into the ball, stopping its movements.

Izzie somersaulted over the girls and landed firmly in front of Professor Grant. Annabelle walked over and grabbed Izzie by the wrist, pulling her hand high up into the air.

"Not only did Izzie win, but she also broke the school record by four seconds! Everyone cheer your classmate on. Those were some pretty sick moves."

"I don't know about the moves." Izzie laughed. "But that was some freaking luck."

She tossed the rubber ball to Professor Grant, who jumped when the ball gave one last twitch before falling asleep in her hands. The entire class clapped and rushed forward, slapping Izzie on the shoulder. She was not only the longest-lasting person on the ball for the girls, but for the boys too, and that made her super proud. She couldn't remember ever playing that game or the toned-down human version of it. The game was just a literal expression of the way she managed her life—clawing at things until they opened.

25

At dinner, the whole cafeteria buzzed with talk about Izzie's amazing feat during gym class. She wasn't used to being the center of attention—at least not the good kind—and she beamed ear to ear with pride. Even Ethan was impressed, having watched her from the other side of the field with the boys.

"You should have seen it, Peter. She was being tossed back and forth, and then *BAM*! She was riding the ball like it was a bull-riding competition. I half-expected her to put her hand over her head and wave it around."

"Man, the one day I had to miss class, and something awesome happened. Congrats, Izzie! That record has stood for seven years. Now everyone is going to try to break your score by the end of the year."

"If they do, they can have it. That was pure luck."

"It was pretty impressive," Luke said from behind her.

She turned around and smiled at Luke, surprised to see

him. He looked at the others, then at the table of jocks on the other side of the room.

"We're talking about tomorrow's practice, but tomorrow morning I'd really like to have breakfast with you guys."

"Sure." Izzie smiled.

"Yeah, man," Ethan replied. "Whatever suits your schedule. You are quite the popular one now."

Luke tried to smile at him, but he knew Ethan was being sarcastic. He sighed and nodded at Izzie, then made his way over to the jocks' table. Izzie glared at Ethan, then grabbed a piece of sausage and folded it up in a napkin. The girls all stood up, feeling the tension, and grabbed their scraps as well.

"Awe where are you guys going?"

"We have a friend to visit." Kathleen huffed.

The girls left the mansion and headed to the shaded part of the forest, bringing their dragon some breakfast. Izzie was still pissed at how irritating Ethan could be, but she tried to be understanding at the same time. Still, Luke had wanted to sit with them; that had to count for something.

When they reached the cave, they called and called for him, but he wasn't there. They tracked his small prints through the moist leaves all through the forest, looping back around to where the cave was. They had learned from Horace that to even have a chance of him appearing they had to call to him in soothing tones. Alison could tell by the large magical energy signature around the cave that he had grown quite a bit, but that was to be expected.

After about an hour of searching and calling to him, he

finally ran out of the bushes. He'd grown to the size of a Saint Bernard, and he just about knocked Izzie down when he jumped on her and sniffed her jacket pockets. He knew they had brought him treats—something they tried to do as often as they could.

"He's bigger every time we visit." Emma laughed as he raced over to her, licking the side of her face.

"I'm going to go make sure there is no one around." Kathleen nodded. "We can't be too careful."

It was true. The dragon not only was not allowed to be with one of the magical beings, but it was also illegal to have one on Earth—a law instituted by the magical community. The last thing they needed was for some of their classmates—like the older girls who picked on them all the time—to find out about him.

The girls opened their napkins and laid the food out in front of him. His eyes grew wide, and he licked his lips as he sat down and sifted through the feast. While he would eat almost anything, today they realized that he really loved brussels sprouts. They never brought him anything other than sausages or bacon for meat, since half the reason he loved small game was the chase.

"So, are we going to name him soon?" Kathleen asked coming back from the surrounding woods.

"Yes," Emma announced. "He actually told me what his name was."

"Okay..."

"His name is Dorvu, which means 'one who under-stands the ways of a dragon.'"

"Dorvu," the others repeated quietly.

"That's a great name." Aya smiled, patting him on the head.

They sat and watched as he finished every last morsel of food and burped, causing a small bit of smoke to waft from his throat. They knew it wouldn't be long until he could breathe fire, but they were nervous that he wouldn't be able to control it. Right then, though, they enjoyed hanging around him until the sun went down.

When the napkins were cleaned up, Izzie picked up a stick and waved it in front of the dragon. She threw it as hard and far as she could and watched, laughing, as he bounded through the leaves to try to catch it. When he returned, he leapt at Izzie, who promptly lost her footing and fell on her face. The dragon pounced on her and bugled a sweet song, having fun being around his clan. Emma couldn't help but feel bad for him, though. His species always congregated into clans, with no real leader. Dorvu had a clan; it just didn't have any other dragons.

Still, she wasn't going to leave him all alone. They'd found him before he'd even entered the world, and they would be there until he no longer needed a clan. Emma walked over giggling and helped Izzie back to her feet. She laughed as she helped pull the wet leaves from her shirt and pants. The girls stayed there all evening, letting Dorvu run wild around them. At one point he disappeared for about ten minutes, coming back with a dead squirrel. He set it in front of Kathleen.

She forced a grin and carefully picked the animal up by the tail, grimacing at the teeth marks in its head. She put the squirrel back down and patted Dorvu on the head, thanking him for the gift. He jumped up on his hind legs and walked to the center of the circle the girls had pulled themselves into. He shook his scales, flashing colors like a puddle of oil on a hot sidewalk. As he shook the dragon morphed, and everyone stared in amazement. Their dragon now looked like a small child.

"Holy crap," Emma said. "He has learned how to morph. He looks like a little boy! That's crazy."

Dorvu walked over and sat down in Kathleen's lap. His wild curly brown hair tickled her chin, and she squeezed him tightly. Izzie shook her head in disbelief.

"After Horace told us what species he was, I looked up the information in the library, but it didn't say anything about dragons being able to turn into humans."

Um, totally. Maybe you should have read a little deeper.

"Whoa." Kathleen shook her head. "He looks like an actual boy, but did you guys just hear that, or am I going crazy?"

"Not crazy," Alison added. "He is a dragon, probably one of the most powerful magical beings in history, and yes, we can all hear him when he talks. Unfortunately, he has spent so much time around us inside his egg that 'teenage girl' is the language he learned."

You ladies are going to be so surprised when I get bigger. I can change into all kinds of different things. In reality, I could walk straight into a crowded city, and no one would even look at me funny.

They sat there surrounding this scaly creature, listening to him talk to them telepathically. He seemed like an adult, even though he wasn't even close to a year old. He spoke with excellent grammar, understood them very well, and even his eyes looked like deep brown human eyes.

The sun is starting to go down. You should get back. They will be looking for you.

"I agree," Alison replied. "We don't want to bring any suspicion to you. Is there anything we can bring you?"

No, thank you. I have all I need right here, and if I get hungry, there is enough small game to feed me for the remainder of the time I stay here. It is nice having visitors, though.

Alison and the other girls said goodbye to the dragon before heading back to the mansion. It wouldn't be long until they'd have no problems finding him, but then again, anyone else with even half a brain could see a giant dragon smashing trees in the distance too.

Alison stared out at the energy moving over the grounds as she laid in her bed that night. She thought about Brownstone and their vacation, even though it had been a bust and had ended before it really began. Up to that point, though, it had been great, and she liked having a family again, and someone she wanted to call Dad.

She smiled, not knowing how in the world she had ended up so lucky. She'd spent years dealing with some of the hardest circumstances any kid her age could imagine, but she wasn't going to complain. Just then a rush of magic hit her chest. She sat up, looking toward the energy floating along the ground. Standing out front of the house was Dorvu. There was something about that dragon that drew her in. It had been that way since he was in his egg.

In the library, she had looked up Drow and dragons. She'd learned that even though there were moments that they worked side by side, both species were incredibly independent creatures. She put her hand up to the glass and the dragon pushed the energy through it, making sure Alison could see it. Vibrant colors swirled through it and made it very simple for her to watch as he turned and bounded back for the woods.

Alison smiled and laid back down, pulling her covers up over her shoulders and resting her eyes. She wanted to wake Izzie up so she wasn't sitting there in the dark on her own, but she knew Izzie'd had some stressful but exciting days and really needed her sleep. The less sleep she got, the more unpredictable her magic became. That was a trait Alison shared, except it was with meditation. Sometimes she wished she could close her eyes like the other girls and drift off into sleep, but then again, she knew that her most precious memories occurred in the wee hours of the morning. She wasn't willing to give that up.

The wind began to pick up outside, and the empty tree branches swayed from side to side. Horace had done an admirable job keeping the courtyard clean through the fall, and now anticipation for the first snow flowed through the entire mansion. Alison loved all the seasons, but this was extra special for her. It would be her first Christmas and Thanksgiving with Brownstone as her official dad. It was going to be an amazing winter, and all she had to do was try to stay out of trouble.

26

I zzie and Alison were anxious and excited all at the same time. They'd waited until the other girls were asleep before huddling together at the window of their dorm room. The crunching leaves and jack-o-lanterns had been replaced by perfect white snow. It glittered and almost glowed beneath the light of the moon. They listened to the sound of the winter wind whipping through the hills, whistling as it jetted past the window.

They had hoped it would snow before they left for winter break and Christmas. The first flakes had started to fall shortly after dinner. They had waited impatiently as the first flake turned into thousands, and those thousands into millions of small powdery ice crystals, each one hand carved by Mother Nature. Izzie did her best to describe the landscape's beauty. She told Alison about the small tracks below leading to a snowman the upperclassmen had built before going to bed that night, but the rest of the property sat untouched like a pure white canvas waiting for an artist.

"It's so beautiful here in the winter," Izzie whispered. "Cold as anything, but absolutely dazzling. I'd never even heard of Charlottesville until I came to school here, and had no idea it was this gorgeous treasure tucked back in the middle of open fields and pastures."

"I understand completely. I've been in snow before, having been to New York so many times, but nothing like this. In my mind, fresh snow is the stuff on your front porch nobody has stepped on yet." Alison laughed. "Here, fresh snow is everything between and around you."

"Are you excited for Christmas this year? I know it's your first one with Brownstone as your official father."

"I am, but I don't expect anything more than last year. I came to the realization that unless I get crazy in the kitchen, which I don't see happening, Christmas Eve ribs and Christmas pizza are going to become my new tradition. It's cute, though, and it warms my heart to know I've come far enough to have traditions with someone other than my mother. I know she is looking down from wherever she is, and she's happy about who decided to take me on. God knows I can be a serious handful."

"You?" Izzie feigned shock. "Not you. You are the epitome of an angel."

They covered their mouths and held back laughter, trying not to wake the others. Izzie smiled, watching Alison sense the energy of the snow floating toward the ground.

"How do you sense snow?"

"Everything gives off energy, magical or not, and snow gives off pure white light."

"Wow, so when it snows like this, you see the world covered in a blanket of light. That is so peaceful. I love it. Oh, I got you a present."

Izzie tiptoed back around her bed and opened her drawer, pulling out a wrapped oblong gift. She placed it in Alison's hands, and Alison ran her hands over it and smiled.

"You got me something?" She walked over and pulled her blanket back, revealing a small wrapped box. "So glad I decided to get you something too."

Alison handed the box to Izzie. "Sorry about the wrapping. Come to find out blind girls lack one superpower: wrapping gifts."

"Please, I am sighted, and I *still* can't wrap gifts."

"You have no excuse." Alison giggled. "Okay, okay you go first. Don't leave me in suspense."

Izzie held the box next to her ear and shook it, smiling as Alison waited patiently. Alison laughed, hearing the crinkling of the paper. "I knew you would shake it, so I put stuffing in it to keep you from being too slick this morning."

Izzie smiled and ripped the package open, making Alison laugh. She pulled the long lid off the small narrow box, folded back a piece of tissue paper, and gasped. Inside was a bracelet, one with red rubies from Ruby Falls cut perfectly and placed on every other link. On the last one, there was a small heart charm with the inscription BFF Forever, including the braille equivalent underneath and their initials on the back.

"Oh, Alison, I absolutely love it. Seriously, it's so beautiful; nicer than anything anyone has ever given me. Of course, I don't remember a lot of my past, so you are lucky." She giggled. "Now you."

Alison rubbed the package along her cheek and took a big whiff. "It's a monkey. I *knew* you would get me one."

Izzie laughed, shaking her head. "If it's a monkey, it's the world's smallest one."

Alison smiled and quickly ripped through the paper and tossed it on the floor. She lifted the lid off and pulled out a small silver bar with a long chain attached to it. She ran her fingers across the bar, reading the braille. It said Sisters for Life, and Alison had to hold back tears. She loved it. It was absolutely perfect.

"Oh, Izzie, this is the best gift ever. It seems we were of the same mind."

"Okay, I want you to turn it over. I am not sure this will work, but I thought it was worth a try. I knew you could see the energy of magic, so I had the same words etched with magic on the other side."

Alison tipped her head to the side and flipped the silver bar over, holding it up to her face. She could see the magic's blue glimmering energy. It was so perfectly done that the energy spelled out the words. Alison gasped quietly and put her fingertips to her lips. She had never seen anything spelled out before.

She leaned forward and hugged Izzie tightly, handing her the necklace. "Put it on me, please. I want to wear it always."

Izzie took the necklace and Alison turned around, pressing the silver against her skin as Izzie buckled the clasp. She smiled and turned back around, still pressing her fingertips against it. She reached her hand out and took the bracelet, finding Izzie's wrist and snapping it on. The two girls sat in front of the window quietly for several moments, enjoying the silent gratitude and feeling of family that coursed through them.

"Now when you sit down for Christmas dinner with Mara, you'll know you aren't an orphan anymore. You have a sister," Alison choked out.

"And you will know the same," Izzie whispered, tears in her eyes.

She took a deep breath and wiped the tears away, laughing. "Let's not dilly-dally, then. The fresh powder is waiting for us."

The girls threw their trash away and started getting dressed, donning the Christmas sweaters Brownstone and Shay had sent them over their pajamas. Alison's sported a Christmas flamingo wearing sunglasses, and Izzie's had a big tree and Santa on the front. Alison couldn't see them, but Izzie couldn't help but chuckle at how ridiculous they looked. They pulled their snowsuits on over the whole ensemble.

Once their boots were on, they put on their winter coats. Izzie pulled Alison's fuzzy hat and gloves from the closet and handed them to her while she grabbed her own. They were dressed for the Arctic, but they knew how cold it got out there on the hills in the winter time. The breeze that rolled through was enough to chill them to the bone.

"Are you ready?" Izzie whispered.

"Sure. I mean you could roll me down the stairs. I am so padded I wouldn't even feel it."

"I think we should try that next year. I don't want to send you back to LA for winter break with broken bones. Your new dad might not appreciate that."

"Good point. I'll use my feet, then." Alison smirked.

"You sure you want to brave this?"

"Double sure. We have to keep up our ritual, and if we planned correctly, I'm hoping we will find Horace up by his cabin with his firepit going. Then we can warm our toes and give Horace the gift we got him before we leave."

"Awesome," Izzie replied. "A little wind, snow, ice, cold, and winter weather won't stop us!"

As they headed out of the dorm and down the stairs, they passed several students roaming the halls enjoying a hot cup of chocolate. When they reached the bottom, Izzie told Alison to wait there. She hurried inside the cafeteria and returned with a tall thermos full of hot chocolate.

"Here, put this carefully in my bookbag," Izzie whispered, turning around.

"Perfect idea. I knew I kept you around for something."

They loaded up and walked out into the courtyard, crossing to the top of the first hill. Izzie shook her head at the beauty of the untouched sparkling snow. They giggled as they slid down to the bottom on their butts. They did this over and over, making their way to Horace's cabin on the other side of the property.

Before they even got there, they smelled the burning oak wood that Horace used, and Alison could hear the crackling of the fire across the fields. They followed the sounds until Izzie could see the fire in the distance. When they arrived, Horace laughed at the girls.

"I figured the snow wouldn't keep you away."

"Are you kidding?" Izzie chuckled.

"Yeah, blizzard warning be damned, we had to see our friend Horace."

"I'm glad you came. I put up two chairs for you."

The girls sat down, and Izzie pulled her bag in front of her. She removed the thermos and the messily-wrapped package that was now smashed in the bottom of her bag. She giggled and handed it to Horace.

"This is from us. Sorry it got smashed."

Horace chuckled, taking the package. "Thank you. Smashed is just as good as not."

"Unless it's a banana." Alison winced.

"Well, let's hope it's not a banana, then." Horace tore into the paper.

"Oh, wow—the new magical thermal-wear gloves! Thank you so much."

"Yep." Izzie smiled. "They will keep your hands warm in weather down to twenty below, and are super-lightweight and thin, so you don't struggle to do things with those thick gloves on."

"We didn't want you to have any excuse for not working." Alison giggled.

"You must have spoken to Mara," Horace joked. "But no, thank you so much, they are perfect."

Izzie opened the hot chocolate while Horace passed around paper cups, taking some of the warmth for himself. He took a deep breath and looked into the fire, watching the flames dance like the faeries in the fall.

"Tell us stories about growing up with your Aunt Estelle," Izzie requested. "They always put me in the perfect mood."

27

The last couple of days of school before Christmas break were always packed full of fun but educational things. For the sophomore class, this included their second integration field trip with the students they had met before at the restaurant. None of the group were ecstatically happy about this, because they knew that the students were very aware of their magic. They had kept their promises, though, not telling anyone—or at least not anyone of importance—that the school was actually for magicals.

The sophomore class packed onto the bus all bundled up in their winter uniforms and boots, hats, scarves, and gloves. They took the jitney across Charlottesville to visit Monticello, the historic home of Thomas Jefferson, his slave concubine, and their children. When they arrived, the human students were already there, shaking from the cold as they waited for them on the front lawn.

The boy and his friends instantly made a beeline for Ethan and the group, greeting them warmly. No one mentioned their shared secret, at least not at first. They grouped off to tour the house, only half listening to the tour guide in the front.

"There are a total of forty-three rooms in the entire complex—thirty-three in the house itself, four in the pavilions, and six under the South Terrace. Jefferson and his wife lived in the main house, and the slaves lived in separate quarters, including the famous Sally Hemmings. She started as Jefferson's mistress in France and came here under one of the most notable slave negotiations in history. She ended up bearing several of Jefferson's children through the years, who were all eventually given their freedom by their father."

"Hey," the boy whispered, elbowing Ethan. "This would be the perfect place for you to try out a little of your magic."

"They would catch me in a heartbeat." Ethan chuckled.

"Nah, you could make it look like a ghost. Just switch out some of the plants in the gardens, or make the dumbwaiter go up and down on its own—something that they will find creepy but not really think about being magical."

"I really shouldn't. If I get caught, it counts against me for graduation when I'm a senior, and let's face it—with my history of practical jokes and two years still ahead of me, I don't need any more black marks on my record."

"Come onnnn," the boy whined. "We're the boring humans. Imagine going to your school day in and day out, but without magic."

"That sounds like torture." Ethan grimaced.

"Welcome to our lives. Nothing but science, math, studying, and the occasional boring-as-hell field trip."

Ethan was tempted. He knew that meeting students like them had to put a spark in the humans' step, but was it worth him possibly getting caught? April Fool's was a no-brainer—totally worth it. The book that had come to life was hands-down worth every second, but this? It would have to be something absolutely awesome to be worth the trouble he'd get into.

Luke walked along with Izzie as she read all the plaques and listened intently to the guide. She really liked historical stuff like that; she always had. Luke, on the other hand, was there because he had to be. The integration class was a requirement for graduating. Luckily for him, he was a shifter. Unless something went terribly wrong, there was no way he could accidentally do magic around the other students.

He actually kind of liked hanging out with them. They treated him normally, like anyone else. They had no idea he was a wolf shifter, and not a single person from the other school ridiculed or picked on him. At one point, he'd considered transferring to a human school, but then he realized withholding his secrets from everyone would be worse than dealing with the people poking fun at him.

"Okay, let me think," Ethan whispered. "It has to be something good. Something that is worth me getting in trouble."

Luke lifted an eyebrow and took a step closer to Ethan. It looked like peer pressure was rearing its ugly little head, and Ethan was going to crash and burn. Luke took another step and laid his arm over Ethan's shoulder.

"Hey, buddy, what are you guys talking about over here?"

Ethan opened his mouth, but the boy answered first. "Ethan is going to do some hilarious magic out here to mess with everyone."

"You are, are you?"

"I was thinking about it." Ethan sulked, knowing he had been had.

"Here's the deal with that, Ethan is one of my best friends, and what happens to Ethan happens to me too. I don't think I can stand by and let him get in so much trouble that he might have to repeat his sophomore year. And for what? To entertain some kids who can't do magic. It's just not logical to me. Come on, Ethan, come check out the carriage house with me. This kid doesn't care if you get in trouble or not."

"I'll tell everyone you are magical," the boy threatened, looking irritated.

Luke leaned toward him. "And then we will wipe all of your memories, and I'll make sure to arrange for you to be doing something most embarrassing when you snap out of it."

The boy gritted his teeth and watched as they walked away, knowing there was nothing that he could do to change Ethan's mind. Alison had listened to them talking. She wasn't sure how well the whole integration thing was going, since one of the humans had tried to talk Ethan into doing something stupid within the first thirty minutes of the tour.

She shook her head and sighed as Tanner grasped her hand in his. She smiled, turning her face toward his bright and shimmering soul. She reached into her pocket and pulled out the Christmas present she'd slipped into her coat pocket before they left. It was difficult to get any sort of privacy at the school, so she'd hoped to find a moment during the field trip to give it to him.

"The construction of the house began in 1769, but it was not completed until 1784. The work on a new design for remodeling and enlarging the house began in 1796 and was completed by 1809. All the bricks in the building were made at Monticello, and the same goes for the nails used to remodel the house. Even the structural timbers mostly came from Jefferson's private land, and the décor was imported from Philadelphia. The glass came from Europe and everything else from Jefferson's estates. He also made sure that the majority of the work was completed by local masons, carpenters, and bricklayers. It was a huge project for the people of Charlottesville and provided some much-needed work at the time. Now, if you'll look over here..."

The tour guide led the group down another hall, and Alison saw her opportunity. She tugged Tanner's hand and asked him to find them somewhere private for a moment. He led her into the living room of the historic home, and she handed him the package.

"I wanted to find a moment alone to give you your Christmas gift. I found it in the kemana, and I thought of you."

He smiled and took the package, peeling the paper off quietly. He tilted the box, and a pocket knife slid out. She'd had his initials engraved on the handle. He held it and smiled, then leaned forward and pressed his lips against hers, taking her breath away for a moment.

"I love it," he whispered, pulling back from her. "I really do. I'll cherish it always. Thank you."

"You're welcome." She smiled happily.

"And it just so happens that I got something for you too, but I didn't bring it with me. When we get back to the school, we'll find a minute together."

"You didn't need to do that, but I would love to spend a minute with you."

He chuckled and touched under her chin to tilt it up and kissed her one last time. "We better get back, or they will notice."

"Oh yes. Heaven forbid we are not fully engrossed in the life and history of Thomas Jefferson." She giggled.

He squeezed her hand, sliding his gift and the wrapping paper carefully into his coat pocket. They rejoined the others, and walked through the house holding hands and just enjoying being near each other. They stayed by each other's side the rest of the trip. When the tour was over and lunch had been eaten, they climbed back onto the bus to head back to the school. Alison pulled her bag into her lap and looked over in surprise as Tanner slid in next to her. Usually, Izzie sat with her, but she could tell from the excitement in his energy that he was there for a reason.

They stayed quiet until the bus pulled away and everyone was focused on their own doings. Tanner reached in his bag and slid a small gift bag into her lap. She felt the bag, wondering if it was her Christmas present from him. With a smile on her face, she pulled out a small box and opened it. She ran her fingers over the small disk inside, feeling the lettering.

"It's a Ruby Falls coin," he whispered. "It's been charmed for good luck, and has the date when we first met and the date of this Christmas on it. They say if you keep it in your pocket, the person who gave it to you will always have you on their mind."

"Uh oh, you may become distracted." Alison giggled.

"I know it's not terribly romantic, but I want you to always be safe, always be lucky, and think of me every time you stick your hand in your pocket."

Alison's mouth curved into a smile and she put both hands on his strong jaw. She kissed him sweetly, first on the lips, then once on the nose. She could feel his eyelashes flutter against her skin, and it sent butterflies into her stomach.

"I love it. It's seriously the perfect gift from you."

"Good," Tanner exclaimed, pleased. "I am not usually a very good gift giver."

"I like how you admitted that after you gave me the present."

"Well, you know, I had to put that out there in case you hated it. Give it sentimental value."

Alison giggled as she put the coin in her pocket, then reached over to take his hand. They rode along the bumpy, winding road in silence for several moments before Tanner turned toward her.

"I was wondering...are you planning on going to the Christmas mixer?"

Alison smiled. "I am. We were all going to go as a group."

"Excellent, then I guess I will see you there. You will have to save me a dance."

"My card is mostly full, but I'll see what I can do." She laughed. "You can have every slot on the card if you would like it."

"I have to admit, that would make me very happy. I don't really want to share you with anyone."

Alison's heart fluttered, and she squeezed his hand tighter. "Funny you should say that, because I feel exactly the same way."

28

Mara Berens sighed as she walked into her office and pulled off her coat. It had been a long morning, taking the class to Monticello, but she was proud of them. Not a single incident, even when left to their own devices. At the beginning of the tour, she had been a little nervous, seeing that twinkle of mischief in Ethan's eye as he whispered with one of the boys from the prep school. But when Luke led him to another part of the house, she assumed she'd made it through another near-crisis by the skin of her teeth.

She put her purse on the desk and sat down behind her computer to pull up her email. Most of it was either junk or things that didn't need to be taken care of until the break. There was one email, though, from a contact of hers in Charlottesville. They were worried. Some of the elves had sensed more dark magic moving toward or inside of the town. They wanted her to come out and do a sweep.

They hoped that whoever it was had left as quickly as they had arrived.

Mara leaned back in her chair and rubbed her chin, thinking about the dark magic trail Izzie had found out of nowhere. Her magic was progressing at a speed that Mara wasn't sure she could manage on her own. It would only be a matter of time before Izzie found out the truth regarding who she was, and who her parents were. While Mara had known she wouldn't be able to keep it a secret forever, she hadn't thought it would come to light that soon.

She glanced at the box on her shelves and sighed, walked over, picked it up carefully, and placed it on her desk. She swished her wand at her door closing it and locking the handle. She waved her wand over the box, whispering the spell to open it. When she heard the clunk of the lock's release, she slowly lifted the lid and stared down at the three memory balls inside. The dark spots pulsing on them had grown. The orbs now showed more darkness than light. She sighed and shut the lid, rubbing her face again.

She had never seen anything like it before, and had no idea what it meant for Izzie's parents or Izzie herself. She was trying very hard to protect Izzie, but she couldn't slow down the progression of her magic. Her only option was to keep Izzie close and make sure that no one in the dark community had access to her. She had sensed some confusion in Izzie the past few weeks, and she wondered if the spell was losing its efficacy. Castings like that didn't last forever, but what concerned her was what would happen to Izzie once she remembered. Those memory balls weren't covered in darkness for nothing.

Mara yawned and stretched her arms high as she waited for her soup to heat up in the microwave in the staff room. She had been dabbling with cooking, and her first attempt at Squash and Corn Chowder had been absolutely amazing. She had jarred up the leftovers, given some to Professor Fowler, and brought the rest for her lunch. The food from the cafeteria was starting to give her indigestion.

She walked over to the window and looked at the field where the students were practicing Louper. They wore their virtual reality headsets and moved all over the pitch. She smiled, remembering when the first SNM Louper team had won a championship. The feds had swarmed them, wanting to know all about the game, and telling them to keep it up. The money they made had been well spent on maintenance and remodels of the property.

One of her favorite things to do was sit in the stands during a Louper game in the warm, crisp spring air rooting for her teams and just enjoying the sport. In reality, she didn't really care about the money it brought the school. She loved the comradery it created. She watched Luke high-fiving other players, laughing, and joking with people who had gone out of their way to bully him during freshman year because he was a shifter. The game brought people together and helped to take away some of the stigmas that the kids dealt with on a regular basis in high school. She only hoped that Luke stayed himself and didn't let their negative influence overcome him.

The microwave beeped, and she walked over and used a

towel to pull the bowl out. She stirred the soup, grabbed the crackers, and headed to her office to enjoy her lunch in peace and quiet. She set her bowl down and laid a napkin across her lap, then blew on a spoonful of hot soup and took a bite, closing her eyes and savoring the flavor. The shuffle of feet in the hallway caused her to pause, and she watched two arguing young men walk by.

"I don't really care what his political affiliation is. I think we have a duty to support the candidate running for governor because he is the first openly magical wizard to run for the seat."

"That makes no sense. You elect officials based on their credentials, and if their beliefs closely align with yours. This guy might be a wizard, but that doesn't mean he believes in truth and justice the way others do."

The day went by fast, and before they knew it, people were heading to the talent show. It was a huge affair, and the entire school was attending. Alison had finished getting ready. She had let Kathleen smooth her hair back into a low ponytail with a red ribbon tied around it. Alison arrived at the auditorium early, and now stood backstage and tried to wait patiently for the event to begin. It was a packed house.

She listened to the different acts as they performed. The first student up was a magic act that included a dog his parents had brought through a portal for the event. He was funny and made the audience laugh, especially when the dog answered any question the student asked. The next couple of acts were comedians, some funny and some not, but the kids in the audience were good sports about it, laughing even when they struggled to find the humor. The next performer was a bit off, and Alison could hardly figure out what was going on.

The boy had come out as a tap dancer, using his wand to create symbols in the air as he danced across the stage. The problem was, his wand was just a little off, and it sent him running all over the stage. By the end of it the teachers had to come up and calm the magic down, and they let the boy know that acquiring a new wand would probably be the safest route before he came back after winter break.

"All right, a round of applause for Troy and his magically tapping feet."

The audience applauded gamely, still thrown by the mess they had just witnessed.

"Next up is Alison, a sophomore who will be singing the great jazz tune *Round Midnight* by Thelonious Monk."

The crowd clapped, and Alison heard Kathleen and Ethan cheering from somewhere in the middle of the crowd. She walked to the center of the stage and stood in front of the microphone, just like during rehearsals, and cleared her throat. She felt a bit more than nervous. Her stomach was doing flip-flops, and her heart beat wildly. She scanned the audience, seeing all the excited energy out there. By that point, everyone knew she was blind, and she could make out a few whispers as people marveled at how well she got around.

It made her even more nervous, but at the same time, she knew they would be kind if she completely sucked. She scanned the front row and found Izzie's happy energy sitting next to Tanner's familiar swirling soul. She could see that he was proud of her but nervous for her at the same time.

Izzie sat forward in her chair and waited until Alison was just about ready to start singing. She pulled in enough energy to create a tiny spell, and discreetly flicked her finger. Alison was immediately surrounded by dancing lights. She knew her friend would be able to see the magic's energy, and she wanted her to remember the night she had sung for the faeries. Alison looked around at the shimmering energy and smiled, thinking immediately about Izzie and the fae. She took a deep breath and relaxed, nodding as the piano started to play.

"It begins to tell 'round midnight
'Round midnight..."

The crowd was silent as they listened to her bluesy voice sing the song with ease. She closed her eyes and swayed her shoulders, listening to the chiming of the piano keys. She felt right at home up on that stage and stopped worrying about all the people in the audience.

She opened her eyes, grabbed the mic, and growled melodically into it. It was one of her favorite songs; the one her mother would hum whenever she was doing dishes, cleaning, or taking care of her. She could remember her mother's deep sultry voice singing her to sleep at night, and she suddenly felt like her mother was there with her on the stage singing along.

The piano went into a longer solo performance as Alison breathed deeply, letting go of her inhibitions and fear. She jumped right in on the last two verses, almost sad that the song was coming to an end. She put her hands by her sides and tapped her leg as she closed her eyes.

"Let our love be safe and sound
When old midnight...comes... around...."

The song ended with just a few extra notes on the piano. The whole room was absolutely silent, and she slowly opened her eyes, wondering if they liked it. Before panic set in, the whole room jumped to their feet and exploded in applause and cheers. Alison chuckled, smiling widely and bowing. She brought the house down. Ethan ran down the aisle and tossed her a bouquet of flowers that everyone had chipped in on. Alison saw him coming and smelled the blooms just before she saw the flicker of energy flying toward her. She caught them and waved again, taking her leave from the stage.

29

The band on the stage in the grand dining hall rocked out. They were a group of older students who were pretty popular amongst the students, covering all the latest hits of Earth music and throwing in a couple of songs of their own. It was finally time for the Winter Mixer, the last big hoorah before the students headed off for their Christmas break. The whole place had been elaborately decorated, including a ton of the Christmas trees that Horace spent so much time growing each year. They were his pride and joy. He had decorated each and every one of them himself.

The tables had all been cleared out, and the hall was decorated from top to bottom with garlands, ferns, mistletoe, and a huge tree right in the center of the room. Magical lights were strung from floor to ceiling without wires, hovering over the surfaces and glowing brightly from the trees. By the walls floated stockings with every student in the school's name magically written at the top. The ceiling had been glamoured to make it look like it was snowing, and the floor, though clear, looked like you were walking across a frozen pond.

They had gone above and beyond for the mixer. Even Mara had joined in the fun of decorating, putting aside her worries and stress to try to enjoy the holidays. She used to love them so much. As she stood watching the students mill around, she couldn't help but think about Leira as a young girl bounding down the stairs, ready to see what Santa brought her. She smiled at the memory and sent a surge of energy to her granddaughter. She chuckled when she got one in return.

She could only imagine what Yumfuck was doing to prepare for the holidays. They didn't have Christmas on Oriceran, but over the years the troll had really gotten into the season. She suspected it mostly had to do with all the food that came around at that time of year. She still had the Christmas card from last year framed on her shelf in her office. It showed Leira, Correk, and Yumfuck dressed in Santa suits and wearing Santa hats, and Yumfuck had a long white beard. Leira and Correk looked completely out of sorts, and Mara still wondered what Yumfuck had had over them to get them to pose for a picture like that.

Whatever it was, it had to be something good and juicy. Horace walked up next to Mara wearing a well-fitted suit for once, and a bow tie with reindeer on it. He smiled at the decorations, proud of another year's hard work.

"Horace, you did fantastically," Mara gushed.

"Thank you, Ms. Berens. It was my pleasure."

They looked at the door when they heard thundering footsteps. The students were flooding in now, and the dance was about to kick off. Everyone was dressed to the hilt. The boys looked more than suave in tuxedos, and some had added a holiday touch of their own like a red bow tie or reindeer socks. The girls wore floor-length gowns and carried the small nosegays Mara had gifted to every girl in the school just for that event.

Izzie's group walked through the door. Izzie, on Luke's arm, waved at Horace. She wore a long silver-sequined spaghetti-strap gown, silver heels, and a white faux-fur wrap was draped around her shoulders. Sparkly earrings dangled from her ears, and her hair was back in a bun and wrapped with a red ribbon. Kathleen walked beside them in a tight black dress that fit snugly to her hips and flared out at the knees. The fabric underneath was bright red, and her hair was braided down her back. Her look was topped off with very cherry lipstick.

Emma giggled, waved at some of the other students, and held the front of her dress up as she walked. It was green satin and fell loosely to the floor. Her shoes were the same color green, with little red bows embroidered all over them. She had her hair pulled halfway back, and ringlets cascaded over her shoulders. She walked with her arm through Ethan's, surprised that he looked so sharp. He had left his baggy clothes in his room and almost looked like James Bond.

Aya and Peter walked behind them. Aya was wearing a shimmering red gown that was way out of her normal comfort zone. She had put in contacts, and wore satin gloves that reached her elbows. Her hair was down and straight and shimmered under the Christmas lights as she moved. Mara smiled at them and waved. Everyone looked absolutely amazing.

"I wonder where Alison and Tanner are?" Mara whispered.

"They are coming in now," Horace replied, nodding at the door.

Mara put her hands to her mouth and gasped at just how gorgeous Alison looked as she clung proudly to Tanner's arm. Her hair was pulled up on top of her head, and sections had been tucked under to create a perfect silver bow. She wore a long gold dress, sequined from the bottom of the flowing skirt all the way up the sleeves. The dress's wide neckline was cut high across her chest and stopped at the edges of her shoulders. The back of the gown was fashioned from a sheer gold material, letting her skin shine through all the way to the curve of her waist. Her makeup was beautiful, with flecks of gold glitter covering her eyelids and a light shimmering gloss on her lips.

They all looked so grown up. They immediately jumped into the party, dancing with each other, laughing, exchanging little gifts they had picked up in the kemana, and just enjoying each other's company. Izzie was in seventh heaven because Luke danced with her for the entire night. Ethan and Peter made their normal rounds on the dance floor, cutting through couples and dancing the tango to almost every slow song. Emma and Aya stayed near each other, giggling at the upperclassmen who eyed them from across the room.

Emma walked over to the Christmas tree to look at all the beautiful ornaments. David walked up beside her and put his hands in his pockets.

"It's really beautiful, isn't it?"

Emma looked at him for a second and shook her head. "David—I didn't even recognize you! I think it's the first time I've seen you without your hat."

He chuckled and scratched his head. "Yeah, I think it's the first time in school history I've been seen in public without it. My friends were starting to question whether it was a Joe Dirt situation. I assured them my hat was not connected to my skull."

"And you don't have a mullet, which is a plus."

"There is definitely that." He laughed.

"I love Christmas trees. Every year since I was a baby, we've gone out to the Christmas tree farm and picked one out, cut it down, drunk hot cocoa or cider, and decorated it with Christmas music playing in the background. It's one of those traditions that just stuck, you know?"

"We do something similar, but last year my mom bought a fake tree, and it was weird. I don't think she will use it again."

"Aw, that's sad." Emma giggled.

"Hey, I was wondering…would you like to dance?"

Emma looked up at him, slightly surprised, and nodded. Everyone watched in shock as David took her hand gently and led her onto the dance floor. They had never actually considered Emma a girl whom David would ask out, but once they were dancing, they fit together almost perfectly. Izzie, resting her head on Luke's arm, looked at her friend and winked. She was happy to see that the girls were having a good time. Kathleen was dancing with Ethan and they were arguing about something, but that just meant they were growing their friendship. The two argued like an old married couple, but everyone knew they were there for each other.

Alison smiled as she watched Emma's soul excitedly dancing with David's as the energy from the magic in the room glimmered and sparkled around them. She thought it was one of the best nights they'd had so far. It was something she would remember for a long time.

When the song ended Ethan clapped his hands, gathering everyone at the foot of the stage. The members of the Entrepreneurs Club climbed onto the stage, giving the band a break. Peter grabbed the cart that had been positioned to the side and wheeled it over. Grace and David stood up there excitedly, and Ethan took the mic.

"Okay, so just a quick pause in the music. David, Grace, Peter, and I are part of the Entrepreneurs Club, and we have been working all semester on a really cool project."

Peter uncovered the cart, picked up four phones, and handed them out to his teammates. Ethan picked up a small chip and held it up to the audience.

"So, this looks like any other chip, right? Wrong. This little chip here not only holds an incredible number of technological advances, but it also has an unlimited supply of magical energy that pulls like a magnet from whatever kemana you are closest to at the time. Right now, it is pulling magic from Ruby Falls and that huge red stone in the center of the underground city."

Ethan stepped to the side and let Grace take the mic.

"We started to brainstorm ways it could be used that not only interested us, but would interest the world, and that was when David got a video call from his mom."

"She's doing well," David leaned in to add. Everyone laughed.

Grace held up her phone and clicked the On button. The others followed suit and held theirs up to the crowd as well. "This chip mixes technology and magic in a way that will allow you to connect virtually any phone no matter the provider, make, or model, as long as it has video capability. It will put you into a magical grouping that only your friends can see, and is always live unless you turn it off in your settings."

David stepped up to the mic. "This can be used in many situations, from social to professional. Colleges can connect with their teachers. People can stay connected and find out about events as they happen."

"We still have some work to do to get it just right, but we wanted you to be the first to see it," Ethan shouted. "It's the future of connectivity.

The students clapped and cheered, impressed by what they had created. Even Kathleen was impressed, and opted not to give Ethan a hard time even though she really wanted to. When they had cleared the stage, the band came back up and rocked old-school tunes for a change.

The party was a blast and lasted until the early morning. By the time they dragged themselves off the dance floor, bow ties had been undone, jackets were off, and girls were carrying their shoes in their hands. The guys left the girls at the top of the stairs, and Tanner stole one last kiss from Alison under the mistletoe before heading off to bed. The whole thing had been a huge success; another awesome night with an amazing group of people.

30

Izzie and Alison walked back from Horace's cottage, having left a gift on his porch—a little something extra they had picked up to go with the gloves. Alison took a deep breath of the cold air. She was sad to be leaving but happy to be able to see her dad and Aunt Shay. Izzie clung tightly to Alison's arm, her teeth chattering.

"I'm gonna miss you guys," Izzie told her. "But I think we are actually going to have the rest of the family at Mara's house for Christmas, so it won't be so tiresome and boring."

"Does that mean the troll is coming?" Alison giggled.

"Heck yes, and Mara said he will teach me some bad-ass card games."

"Oooh, we'll have to figure out a way to teach me how to play them. Maybe magically imprint the cards or something like you did with my necklace."

"We can figure something out, I'm sure. Do they make braille playing cards?"

"I doubt it." Alison giggled. "Though they make just about everything these days, so I could be wrong. I just feel like they would be incredibly heavy."

Izzie covered her mouth. Alison lifted an eyebrow, looking at her energy. Izzie was trying not to laugh.

"What is it?"

"I was just picturing all of us sitting around a table with thick metal playing cards like we were the Flintstones, but then I realized it was probably a horrible thing to laugh about."

Alison was silent for a moment, which worried Izzie, but then broke out in laughter. "Oh, my God, who would be Bam Bam?"

"Aya, most definitely." Izzie giggled, then let out a deep sigh. "Will you call me while you are gone?"

"Of course, I will. This would be the perfect time for that new invention the club came up with. We could be together for the holidays, even the boring parts, and still be in the places we need to be."

"We will have to work on that for summer vacation."

"Most definitely."

In the foyer of the mansion, they tapped their boots off and joined the others, who were watching Alison's luggage and waiting for her to get back from the walk with Izzie. Ethan jumped down from the stairs and put his arms out.

"Group hug!"

They all laughed and came together in a big hug in the middle of the floor.

"All right, let's get this show on the road." Kathleen clapped. "I got presents to wrap, presents to receive, and eclairs to make with my mother. Izzie, you staying or coming along?"

"I'm coming to see you guys off." She smiled, looking at Luke.

"This is where I leave you guys, then." Tanner bowed.

Everyone booed and hugged Tanner before filing outside. Alison stood in front of him, staring lovingly at his glimmering soul. She kissed him on the cheek.

"I'll see you real soon," he whispered. "And whenever you miss me, just give that coin a rub, and I will know."

"Then I will keep it in my hand the whole time." She laughed.

Tanner kissed her cheek and she waved, then picked up her suitcase and walked out to meet the others. They boarded the bus and talked excitedly about their Christmas plans as they headed toward the Starbucks. Kathleen was jealous that Izzie got to spend Christmas with Yumfuck, but Izzie promised to video-message her with him while they were there.

They went through the fake magical wall in the Starbucks, waved goodbye to some of the other students, and headed down to the platform. The trains arrived one at a time. Each took another one of the group off to their destination. When it was just Alison and Izzie on the platform, Alison gave her a huge hug and squeezed her hands.

"We'll be back before you know it. Don't drink too much eggnog."

"I'll try." She laughed.

Alison climbed onto the train and took a seat by the window as the rest of the crowd boarded. Izzie's energy had streaks of blue sadness running through it. Alison smiled and waved at her, hoping she would at least try to have a good vacation. One day she'd talk Izzie into coming with her to Los Angeles. They'd have a blast out there, and she knew Brownstone and Shay would love her and find her powers interesting.

Part of Alison wondered why Mara was so strict about the places Izzie could go. She treated the girl like she was in some sort of danger or something. From what Izzie knew, she was only the headmistress' ward because there had to be a guardian for her to attend the school and the orphanage couldn't be it. Then again, Alison had been there long enough to know what was known wasn't always the whole truth, and also that it would come out in the end. She hoped for Izzie's sake that it would be a good truth, not any more hurt or confusion. They had both been through too much to have more dropped on them.

She took a deep breath and tilted her head to the side, noticing a dark energy pass behind Izzie. It didn't seem to be a person, because she couldn't detect a soul, not even a dark one. It was more of a magical energy mist. She started to point behind her friend, but the train whooshed out and then she was too far away to catch Izzie's attention. Besides, it had already passed her, and Izzie wouldn't be able to see the energy anyway. She shrugged and hoped that what she had just seen wouldn't return.

As the train whooshed away, Izzie put her hand in the air and waved, then smiled and crossed her arms. Suddenly she felt a chill on her neck that ran straight down her spine. She wriggled her shoulders and looked around, trying to see where it had come from.

The feeling she had been getting sporadically over the last couple of months slammed into her. She wobbled and braced herself on the column next to her, then hung her head and rubbed her temples. Her stomach was churning, and heat bounced around in her chest. More energy slammed through her, and her head flew back, and her pupils turned dark-grey.

She was having another memory or vision or whatever they were. She stood in a dark alley, not much younger than she was now. Streaks of dark magic whizzed by her head and she fought back, returning the fire. There were explosions in the background, and in front of her was a group of men she couldn't quite make out. Whoever they were, they were incredibly powerful, and she had obviously done something to tick them off enough for them to be trying to kill her. To her right and left were the same two people, the man and the woman, both fighting hard. The man held his arm, and blood dripped through his fingers. They felt familiar, but at the same time, they weren't.

As she turned toward the battle, a fireball flew toward her face, blocking her sight. She put up her arms in the vision and braced for impact, but before it plowed into her, she jolted back to reality. Izzie let out a deep breath and her pupils cleared. She was still standing on the platform and was now surrounded by commuters waiting to catch the next train. She rubbed the sweat off her forehead, trying not to look crazy. Everyone was so focused on their phones or tablets that no one had noticed the fit that Izzie had just had. She rubbed her chest until the tightness left and leaned against the column again.

Izzie stood there for quite a while, gathering herself and trying to get the nauseous feeling to leave her stomach. By the time the next train took off, she finally felt in control enough to leave. She pushed off from the column and steadied herself before heading for the stairs. She looked back at the column and the crowd and shook her head.

"What the hell was that?"

Alison changed trains just five minutes away and sat back in her seat, knowing it wouldn't take long to get from there to Los Angeles. It was a straight shot, with only three stops on the route. She pulled her bookbag into her lap and took out Tanner's coin. She held it in her palm and closed her eyes, thinking about him.

"I miss you already," she whispered.

"I miss you too," Tanner replied. His voice was distant, as if it were carried on the wind.

She opened her eyes and looked down at the coin. A small smile moved across her lips. It was like a cell phone, except it was connected through touch and you couldn't have a full conversation. She liked it because it enabled her to feel his energy and have him feel hers. They worked so well together that she missed that energy whenever she wasn't around him.

She felt like it was silly to feel that strongly for someone. She'd never had a boyfriend before, so she had no idea what was normal. She supposed that love was different for everyone. Some people were overwhelmed with emotions, while others were just content to be together. She could only go with her gut instinct with him and hope it led her down the right path.

A bell dinged above her head, and an automated voice announced, "Next stop, Los Angeles. Station Three."

That was Alison's stop. It was the same place she had gotten on the train at the beginning of the year. She dropped the coin inside a small brown velvet pouch, then pulled the strings tight and tucked it safely into her book-bag. By the time she was done the train had begun to slow down, finally coming to a full stop at the station. Alison grabbed her suitcase and followed the others out, stepping to the side and looking around for Shay and Brownstone's souls. She thought for a moment that she had gone to the wrong station. She was about to pull out her phone to call them when she heard Shay yelling her name.

She looked up and found their energies hovering next to each other at the top of the first flight of steps. Alison smiled and raced up the stairs, throwing her arms around Brownstone and Shay at the same time. They hugged her tightly, glad to see her safe. Brownstone took her suitcase, and Shay grabbed her hand.

"Welcome home, Alison," the bounty hunter said.

"Thanks, Dad!"

This is the night before Michael and I released the first book in the Leira Chronicles... one year ago. We had just spent months creating a new universe – the Oriceran Universe complete with amazing artwork and we were all anticipation without knowing how it would all turn out.

What a difference a year makes.

Forty-six books, including Wary is Her Love released on our first birthday, and two short Troll stories later we are just beginning to rock and roll. We've learned a lot along the way like art can be very, very expensive and ask for help, often and from as many talented people as you can find.

Or keep a well-honed sense of humor for when things head south right before a book comes out or even when a book is coming out, or my favorite – even when the wrong book is sent out with the right cover. Breathe, make some phone calls, make a joke or two, let all the fans know and keep going.

But what was the biggest thing I learned this year? Dreams really do come true and if it takes thirty years it's all the sweeter. This was the year I finally became a best-selling author with a wild and wonderful enormous crowd of BEST FANS EVER who can get a book in the morning, read it and review it by the afternoon and send me a message that evening asking when the next one is coming out... Love you all and the stickers and the mugs and the pictures.

Another BIG THANK YOU is for Michael Anderle who asked me if I wanted to write a series with him (he claims) and I heard UNIVERSE (which I still say is what he said) and apparently when I started creating a universe didn't say, what the hell? Instead he quickly invited two writers to join us and I turned around with two of my own. So, thank you to A.L. Knorr, S.M. Boyce, Flint Maxwell and Sarah Noffke for agreeing to join in the fun before we even had a web site and could only describe what we were about to do. Have I mentioned writers are wonderfully crazy?

Favorite funny moment you don't know about... Michael Anderle and I were talking on Zoom, which means our computers were connected and we had a window into each other's houses. We work long hours and some weeks it's 24/7. During one of those weeks, after one of those talks somehow both of us forgot to shut off the connection. Hours later I sat down and wondered why I was still staring at Anderle's living room... wait for it... just as Anderle strolled by drinking a Coke! He stays on brand even when he thinks no one is watching. I had to stop laughing long enough to yell to him like someone stuck in the World In Between to get his attention.

There are also so many people behind the scenes of the Oriceran Universe that you never get to see who do so much to help us get these books to you. BIG THANK YOU to all of the clever people who help to do covers, check copy, keep calendars, post announcements, send out newsletters like Stephen Campbell, the Zen Master who's the man behind the curtain or Jami Crumpton who makes sure you get to see a newsletter or posts on social media. Or our JIT team, the folks who read the books two days before they go live, looking for and suggesting fixes for mistakes that inevitably find their way into all books. The list of people who play an important part goes on and on.

Okay, and here we are a year later and probably appropriately right at the moment I'm sitting in a hotel room – my old house has sold – and I'm waiting for the new house I've been building to finally be ready. I have about three weeks to go – and yes, Anderle, you will touch the upgrades. The bathroom tile has texture, dude. It's my dream house with an amazing office to write a lot more books, give away a lot more stickers, hatch a lot more cool things to do for you guys and just keep going. What a life! Thank you for making this one of the best years of my life. More adventures to follow.

First, THANK YOU for reading this book! That you went through the story and Martha's *Notes* to read mine is a real honor and I appreciate you taking your time to read these musings.

It has been a freaking WONDERFUL ride into this new area of publishing called, "Young Adult."

I have to admit, it's kind of *scary*. Why? Because I don't remember that age very well.

Martha gets the credit for the focus of this series because…well, she *likes* it. We were talking about crafting a series for young adults (you know, two silly authors talking long distance).

One (me) is in the Aria Casino and Hotel, the other is probably pole dancing or something.)

<These are my *Author Notes*. She can make up her own lies in hers… Wait, can I say pole dancing in a YA book?>

MA: "So, we want to try something different."

MC: "Yeah, but what?"

MA: <shrugs shoulders, but Martha can't see this over the phone. We are simply on voice> (which seems so plebeian at the moment.)

MC: "You love this stuff, why don't we go against JK Rowling?"

MA: "Just to confirm we are on the same wavelength, would that be multi-billionaire JK Rowling?"

MC: "Sure. Why not?"

MA: "Beats the <redacted> out of me. It's not like anyone is trying too hard anymore. H@#@, if we even get a tiny sliver of her success, we are *golden*."

MC: "You think we can do it?"

MA: <*Laughing*> "Oh, we can TRY, but whether we sell any books and make something fans like is a whole *other* question."

<Then we talked about other ideas for 15-20 minutes.>

MA: "So, I've been thinking about our earlier conversation."

MC: "Which one? We've had ten."

MA: "The one where we do something to compete with JK Rowling. We might as well go big or go home, right?"

<*Bless Martha's little heart, but she is willing to do the stupidest things with me just because she hates to think she is missing the fun. I've no idea if she still thinks there was fun missing.*>

MC: "SURE!"

MA: "Ok, so we are taking that conversation from a while back about School of Necessary Magic, and we are switching it this way…"

<We talk another thirty something minutes.>

MC: "Done?"

MA: "Done!"

MC: "Ok, so…who's doing beats…"

MA: "This is Young Adult. That's not my area. I cuss too much."

<Pause>

MC: "You *<redacted>*."

And *that* is how Martha became the main driver for *The School of Necessary Magic*. Mind you, I'm not sure if this is actually how it went down, but I like to think this is taken from real life. Important details may have been changed because I don't freaking remember them all.'

Alison is one fun character, and I'm glad you like her!

Ad Aeternitatem,

Michael Anderle

OTHER REVELATION OF ORICERAN UNIVERSE BOOKS

The Unbelievable Mr. Brownstone

* Michael Anderle *

Feared by Hell (1) - Rejected by Heaven (2) - Eye For An Eye (3) - Bring the Pain (4) - She is the Widow Maker (5) - When Angels Cry (6) - Fire with Fire (7) - Hail To The King (08)

I Fear No Evil

* Martha Carr and Michael Anderle *

Kill the Willing (1) - Bury the Past, But Shoot it First (2) - Reload Faster (3) - Dead In Plain sight (4)

School of Necessary Magic

* Judith Berens *

Dark Is Her Nature (1) - Bright Is Her Sight (2) - Wary Is Her Love (3)

Rewriting Justice

* Martha Carr and Michael Anderle *

Justice Served Cold (1) - Vengeance Served Hot (2) - Bounty Hunter Inc (03)

The Leira Chronicles

* Martha Carr and Michael Anderle *

Waking Magic (1) - Release of Magic (2) - Protection of Magic (3)

- Rule of Magic (4) - Dealing in Magic (5) - Theft of Magic (6) - Enemies of Magic (7) - Guardians of Magic (8)

The Soul Stone Mage Series

* Sarah Noffke and Martha Carr *

House of Enchanted (1) - The Dark Forest (2) - Mountain of Truth (3) - Land of Terran (4) - New Egypt (5) - Lancothy (6) - Virgo (7)

The Kacy Chronicles

* A.L. Knorr and Martha Carr *

Descendant (1) - Ascendant (2) - Combatant (3) - Transcendent (4)

The Midwest Magic Chronicles

* Flint Maxwell and Martha Carr*

The Midwest Witch (1) - The Midwest Wanderer (2) - The Midwest Whisperer (3) - The Midwest War (4)

The Fairhaven Chronicles

* with S.M. Boyce *

Glow (1) - Shimmer (2) - Ember (3) - Nightfall (4)

CONNECT WITH THE AUTHORS

Martha Carr Social

Website: http://www.marthacarr.com

Facebook:
https://www.facebook.com/groups/MarthaCarrFans/

Michael Anderle Social

Website: http://kurtherianbooks.com/

Email List: http://kurtherianbooks.com/email-list/

Facebook Here:
https://www.facebook.com/TheKurtherianGambitBooks/